THE SMALL MOSAICS OF
MR. AND MRS. ENGEL

THE SMALL MOSAICS

OF MR. AND MRS. ENGEL

PATRICIA COLLINGE

with drawings by Susanne Suba

Doubleday & Company, Inc., Garden City, New York

All of the stories in this collection originally appeared in *The New Yorker* with the exception of *View From a Closed Window*, which was first published in *Vogue*, and *Dress Rehearsal*.

The Pope that Mr. and Mrs. Engel saw was the late Pius XII. If any of the other characters in these stories seem equally real, the author couldn't be more pleased.

For
Marjorie Benchley, Cynthia and Robert Wallsten
and James Nichols Smith

Mr. and Mrs. Engel

Ladies to the Center

Mr. and Mrs. Engel

WOMEN AND CHILDREN FIRST

When Mr. and Mrs. Engel decided to take a vacation in Europe, they realized that they would be thrown into more weeks of each other's uninterrupted company than they had known for years, but they weathered this contiguousness a good deal better than they expected. They made no particular rules of conduct, but certain compromises established themselves. Mr. Engel was patient about shopping and picture galleries, and in return Mrs. Engel curtailed reading in bed at night and was reasonable about ruins. However, they continued to be themselves, and it was only natural that moments of friction would arise. Indeed, the first one had come as early on as their second day out on the Italian liner that was carrying them on their initial voyage to Naples.

Mrs. Engel had barely got used to the fact that she was actually at sea when the loud-speaker which relayed important information intruded on the peace of the Engels' stateroom to announce that at three o'clock that afternoon all passengers were requested to assemble in the main lounge for boat drill. It repeated this twice in Italian and twice in English, rousing Mr. Engel irrevocably from his post-luncheon nap, and he turned over in his bed, to which he had retired as thoroughly as if for the night, and pulled a pillow over his head. Mrs. Engel, who had merely removed her dress and lain on the outside of her bed under a light cover, sat up straight.

"Boat drill!" she exclaimed. "It was on the day's activities list and I forgot it!"

She looked at her bedside clock. "Two-thirty! Goodness, that doesn't give us much time." She got off her bed and struggled into her dress.

"We have to wear our life jackets," she said. "I know they're around here somewhere." She opened a closet and, straining, pulled down two bulky orange objects from the shelf where they had been packed. "I guess they go on like a waistcoat," she said. She put one on, and tied its broad tapes and looked at herself in the mirror. "I look like a turtle," she said to Mr. Engel, who removed the pillow from his head and sat up wearily. He propped the pillow at his back and reached for a paper-back edition of *The Brothers Karamazov* which lay on the bed table.

"What are you doing?" Mrs. Engel asked him. "You've got to get dressed."

"I'm going to read," said Mr. Engel.

"*Read?* But we have to go to the boat drill!"

Mr. Engel found his place in his book and turned on the light over his bed.

"Aren't you *coming?*" asked his wife.

"I'm going to read for a while," Mr. Engel repeated. "It might put me to sleep again. But you go ahead if you want to."

"It isn't wanting to," said Mrs. Engel, "it's a thing we have to do. It's an order—well, they say 'request' but they expect you to obey."

"If it was an order they'd say so," said Mr. Engel. "They wouldn't fool around."

"Italians are very polite," said Mrs. Engel. "That's why they said 'request' instead of 'you must' or something. I don't understand you," she added, as Mr. Engel made no reply. "When you were in the Navy you were *livid* about discipline, and now you—you just *lie* there!"

"Look," said Mr. Engel, "all you have to know is where your boat station is, and I checked on that yesterday, before we sailed."

"You didn't tell me you'd done that."

"I didn't want you to start worrying about accidents," said Mr. Engel. "I know the way you get."

"Do you know what *I* think," said Mrs. Engel, "I think you don't want to go up there in a life jacket. The way you won't play games."

Mr. Engel ignored this, and she started for the door and then hesitated. "Don't you feel well?" she asked. "Have you a headache?"

"I feel fine," said Mr. Engel.

"Then why won't you come?"

"I told you," said Mr. Engel, "but you go ahead if you want to."

"All right," said Mrs. Engel, "but I still don't understand you. I thought you'd be the *first* to go."

She waited, but Mr. Engel had settled frowningly to his

book, so she went out of the stateroom, and closed the door behind her.

Outside in the passage the preparations for the drill were already under way. The stewards and stewardesses standing at their posts wore life jackets, and so did the passengers dribbling in twos and threes from their cabins. Feeling solemn and civic-minded, Mrs. Engel fell in with them and presently found herself being directed to a seat in the main lounge. She gave the steward the same grave bow of acknowledgment that she gave to the usher when she went to church, and then she sat down and looked about her. For all the seriousness of the meeting, she was surprised to find that the rapidly filling lounge looked gay. Of course, the repeated orange of the life jackets had something to do with it, but if the orchestra were playing, she thought, she might almost be at a ship's gala, or at a fancy-dress party where everyone had come in the same costume. Gradually she became aware that the party spirit emanated from the passengers themselves. Some sat quietly, like herself, and some stood about looking as if they had done this so many times that it had become a bore, but for the most part they were behaving as if it were just one more activity planned for their diversion. There was a fluttering sound of chatter, punctuated with bursts of laughter, as cameras flashed and stout men here and there posed anticly. Stewards and stewardesses smiled indulgently as they sorted their charges into groups. Children giggled and poked at each other, and women wriggled self-consciously in their bulbous jackets. They all seemed to be concerned with how they looked in them, Mrs. Engel thought, instead of thinking of why they had them on, and she began to think about it herself. Suppose it wasn't a drill? Suppose this were a real sinking? How would everyone behave then? How would she behave herself? She knew now that Mr. Engel was safe in the stateroom reading *The Brothers Karamazov*, but suppose this were real, and she didn't know where he was on the boat, and couldn't find him? Suppose the young mother across from her with the three little girls couldn't find her little girls? And if it were real would everyone be trusting and obedient, or would some be struggling and resisting, and would the others be crying, or praying, or perhaps screaming?

An officer came, and Mrs. Engel was led with her group to their station. One of the long windows that enclosed the deck had been removed and the wind blew in from the gap it left, fresh and a little cold, and women clutched at their hair as they were lined there. "Here we go, boys," said a voice from the rear rank. "Hold onto your hats!" There was a ripple of laughter and someone said "hush," but there was still a facetious murmur, only half subdued. Why can't they be serious, Mrs. Engel wondered, and then thought that perhaps they were afraid to be. They were here, though, she told herself regretfully, and not in their cabins reading, and she wished very much that Mr. Engel were beside her now. Then, a shadow fell, blotting out the sky, and slowly, on ropes that whispered, a lifeboat was lowered from the deck above and came to rest in the open space and hung there, empty and waiting. The banter died, and there was a long, queer silence.

Then sailors came to replace the glass, the lifeboat was taken up, and the group was dismissed.

Back in the stateroom Mrs. Engel went to the mirror to tidy her hair.

"Well, how was it?" asked Mr. Engel, who was still in bed reading.

Mrs. Engel did not answer quite at once. "It was very instructive," she said, when she had brushed her hair back to smoothness. "I still don't see why you wouldn't come."

"I told you," said Mr. Engel once more, "I know where our station is."

"You don't know about getting into the lifeboat," said Mrs. Engel. "It comes right down to the deck and all you have to do is step into it. It's wonderful how they have it all arranged." She pushed a wave of hair into place with her fingers. "Only probably your not being there will throw them all off."

Mr. Engel put down his book. "How do you make *that* out?" he asked.

"Well, our lifeboat only holds so many people, so when you weren't there they gave your seat to someone else, I expect. Then if anything happened and you came up with me, you'd be one extra and it would throw them off."

"They know how many passengers they have to take care of, and I wouldn't be in that boat, anyway," said Mr. Engel.

"Of course you would, you're supposed to be with *me*."

Mr. Engel shook his head. "Women and children go first," he said.

"They go what?"

"First," said Mr. Engel, "I thought you knew that."

"I knew it," said Mrs. Engel after a pause, "but I thought that was only long ago. I mean, in the old days before radar and all those things. I didn't think they did it any more."

"Rule of the sea," said Mr. Engel, and went back to his book.

Mrs. Engel turned her hairbrush slowly in her hands. She saw the lifeboat again, waiting at the boat station, and she saw Mr. Engel standing on the deck while she went to safety. She saw him standing looking after her the way he had looked after her on railway platforms the times she had had to go away without him. She saw him the way she always saw him when he wasn't with her, very thin again and a little awkward, the way he had been when she first met him, and she knew she wouldn't get into the lifeboat; she would stay with Mr. Engel. She put down her brush.

"Just the same," she said, "I think when there's a drill people ought to go to it, for *discipline*."

"I'll go next time," Mr. Engel promised abstractedly, from the depths of his reading.

Mrs. Engel put her hairbrush away in the drawer in which she kept it.

"If you couldn't come with me, what lifeboat would you be in?" she asked, as if casually.

"Whatever one they put me in. It would all depend, anyway."

"Depend?"

Mr. Engel put down his book again. "Look," he said, "as far as the lifeboats go, it all depends on how the ship lists."

"Lists?"

"Turns over," said Mr. Engel, "it might go one way or the other. If our station was on the wrong side, we might not be able to get to it, or they might not be able to launch the boats on that side."

"What would they do, then?" asked Mrs. Engel.

"Well, they'd—they'd reassign us," Mr. Engel answered.

"We'd just have to stand by for orders. It's hard to say; you see, when a ship keels over—" He left it unfinished.

"I didn't think about that," said Mrs. Engel.

"Well, don't think about it now," said her husband. "You're in a state already."

"I'm not in a state," said Mrs. Engel. She picked up her life jacket and the one she had taken down for Mr. Engel and stood looking at them. She tried to imagine the ship turned over, its familiar deck a sudden precipice. It would be like seeing the world break into pieces, she thought, with everything you knew and counted on jagged and slivered like a broken mirror. She went to the closet and tried to put the life jackets back on their shelf, but it was too high and she gave up and just held them tight against her.

"It wouldn't matter about the ship listing, anyway," she said then, "because whichever way it went over, or whatever happened, I wouldn't get into one without you."

"Get into what without me?" asked Mr. Engel, who had returned to his reading.

"A lifeboat," said Mrs. Engel.

Mr. Engel looked up and saw her standing facing him, the life jackets clutched in her arms, her heels digging hard into the carpet of the cabin.

"Well, I *wouldn't*," she told him, as if he had spoken.

Mr. Engel said nothing for a moment, and when his reassurance did come only Mrs. Engel could have understood it.

"Oh, well," he said uncomfortably, "neither would I." He put *The Brothers Karamazov* on the bed table. "I think I'll get up," he said. "Want to have tea in here or upstairs?"

Mrs. Engel's grip on the life jackets relaxed. "Upstairs," she said, "only not where the orchestra is. In the little lounge where it's quiet."

"You'd better go on up, then," said Mr. Engel, "and grab a window table."

Mrs. Engel put the life jackets on the end of her bed and eyed them unsurely. "Well, don't be long," she said to Mr. Engel.

When she had gone Mr. Engel dressed with less deliberation than was usual with him. Then, before he left the stateroom himself, he put the two life jackets up on their shelf and pushed them back as far out of Mrs. Engel's sight as he could.

*T*he thing about being on an Italian boat," Mrs. Engel said to Mr. Engel, when they were a few days out on their long, slow voyage to Naples, "is that it's almost like being there right off. I mean, there's Italian going on all around us, and the food is Italian, and the loud-speaker is Italian. It's like a dress rehearsal."

"I thought a dress rehearsal was for something you knew," said Mr. Engel. "We don't know Italy at all yet."

"Well, you know what I mean," said Mrs. Engel. Mr. Engel didn't, but he didn't say so. Instead he remarked that if the barber could take him, he would have his hair cut.

"All right," said Mrs. Engel, "and I'll go up and sit in my deck chair. I've hardly used it yet." She rummaged in one of her bags and brought out an Italian phrase book. "I'll study this, and I'll meet you at lunch."

Mr. Engel came over and took the book and opened it casually. " 'When I see my cousin I shall borrow his bicycle,' " he read aloud.

Mrs. Engel took the book from him. "It's just an exercise in grammar," she said. "They don't expect you to *say* it."

"Why do you bother with it, then?" asked Mr. Engel. "Why don't you just learn the verbs?"

"You'd better see if the barber can take you," said Mrs. Engel. "I'm going up to my chair."

Going to her deck chair was something that in time she would become accustomed to, but now it felt new and exciting, as had everything that had happened since she and Mr. Engel had left New York. The boat was still a thing to be explored, although she was beginning to know it a little. She knew in which lounge one could have a quiet cocktail, and in which there was an accordion player, who might anchor at one's table. She knew where the library was, but she had not found the hours when it was open. She had discovered the chapel, which made her feel more than ever that she was already in Italy. "And it isn't something they set up for Sundays," she told Mr. Engel. "It's a real chapel, and it's always there, and it has a madonna and an altar, and it was just full of flowers. People send their going-away flowers, and if I had only known, I would have sent some of ours. But then," she added, "maybe they only take them from Catholics."

As she became familiar with the ship she began to realize that the life on board was not very different from the life on land. Already, the passengers had become a community, with its attendant cliques and sets. The bridge set, the canasta set, the athletic set that went in for deck tennis and shuffleboard, and carefully counted miles of walking around the decks. The dancing set, and the bar set. But she was still unaware that there was another set of those content to look on and comment. For the most part this was composed of ladies of comfortable widowhood, traveling in pairs, or spinsters glassily denying their loneliness. Mrs. Engel had exchanged greetings with some of them, and occasional remarks about the weather, but since she was almost always with Mr. Engel, acquaintanceship had gone no further.

Now, this morning, when she reached her deck chair, two of these ladies were stretched, reading, in the chairs to her left. Mrs. Engel knew vaguely that one was a Mrs. Amburt, and the other a Miss Orpen, or Orken. Miss Orpen had a thin, pale face that made Mrs. Engel think of pince-nez, while Mrs. Amburt was a handsome, large woman with carefully netted gray hair. They both wore knitted dresses with pearl chokers, but Mrs. Amburt's pearls were real. They acknowledged Mrs. Engel's arrival pleasantly, if absently, and returned to their novels. Mrs. Engel settled in her chair and opened her phrase book. She was just debating with herself as to whether it was worth her while to memorize the Italian for sugar tongs, when she became aware of a stiffening to attention on the part of her neighbor.

"There she is," said Mrs. Amburt, "and I ask you to look at her!"

Mrs. Engel was not sure that she was being addressed directly, but she took off her reading glasses obediently, and looked up to see a young woman coming down the deck, a small boy clinging to her hand, one of the ship's younger officers at her heels. She was neither short nor tall, nor was she especially pretty. She wore a loose sweater and rather rumpled slacks, and no one would have looked at her twice, Mrs. Engel thought, if it hadn't been for her hair, which was a flying mass of chestnut and gold, and a vitality that seemed not so much unrestrained as unleashed. She did not look at the women in the deck chairs as she passed, but Mrs. Engel thought that she slowed a little, as if accepting their examination.

"Absolutely brazen," said Mrs. Amburt, making every syllable distinct. "And did you see that unfortunate child? White as a sheet?"

"It's dreadful," Miss Orpen murmured, "quite dreadful."

"It's disgraceful," said Mrs. Amburt firmly. "What a woman like that is doing with a child at *all* is beyond me. It is obvious that she has only one interest in him; to parade with him and draw attention to herself."

Miss Orpen's pale lips sketched a smile. "She hardly needs a decoy," she said, "I have yet to see her—unattended."

"*Ça va sans dire,*" said Mrs. Amburt. "I doubt if there is a man on board that has escaped her. Passengers or crew."

"I heard her outside my cabin last night," said Miss Orpen, "saying good night to some man. At least I presumed she was saying 'good night.'"

"What I cannot understand," said Mrs. Amburt heavily, "is how a woman like that is traveling first class. Apart from anything else, look at her clothes."

"The world has changed," said Miss Orpen.

"Not that much," said Mrs. Amburt. She turned to Mrs. Engel, conscious that she was listening, wide-eyed.

"My dear," she said, "I assure you, we are deeply concerned. Not about this young woman's morals, or lack of them, but about that wretched little boy. Really, a woman like that is unfit to have the care of a child."

"He looked very clean," said Mrs. Engel.

"Well, I suppose she *washes* him," said Mrs. Amburt, "but he has no *proper* care. Not only does she drag him about with her all day, but she keeps him up with her night after night, playing Bingo. Bingo! And he can't be more than six or seven years old. And when there isn't any Bingo, she keeps him up with her watching the dancing, dead for sleep, his poor little face white as a—as a sheet. And does she send him to the children's dining room where he belongs? Oh, no! She brings him to our dining room, even for late dinner!"

"There's a very nice playroom for the children," Miss Orpen chimed in, "and a nurse in attendance, but she never sends him there, either!"

"I dislike to say it," said Mrs. Amburt with relish, "but I am afraid she uses her child as certain women use a little dog on a leash. To encourage approach."

"Goodness," said Mrs. Engel.

"She's obsessed," said Miss Orpen. "She even talks to the stewards and the sailors."

"Well, I talk to them, too," said Mrs. Engel guiltily.

"Oh, my dear," said Mrs. Amburt, "we all say good morning and good evening to them. But she laughs and jokes with them. I've seen the head steward positively blush."

"But she never even says as much as 'good morning' to a *woman* on board," said Miss Orpen. "It gives such a bad impression."

"It gives exactly the impression she wants to give," said Mrs. Amburt slowly, "and if it weren't for the child I wouldn't even discuss her. I'm an old traveler, and I have learned this much. There's one on every boat."

When Mrs. Engel joined Mr. Engel for lunch she told him all about it. "And she just trails her little boy after her like a little dog. He's in here with her now," she finished breathlessly.

"I don't know who you're talking about," said Mr. Engel.

"Over near the buffet," said Mrs. Engel, "with the loose sweater and the red hair." Mr. Engel glanced in the direction his wife indicated.

"Looks harmless to me," he said.

"I know, that's what *I* would have said," Mrs. Engel agreed. "I always thought a woman like that would be more sort of alluring looking. More like that woman over there."

"Over where?" asked Mr. Engel.

"Under the porthole behind you, with the green earrings.

You can see her if you pretend to be looking for the steward."

Mr. Engel made an unwilling half-turn and saw, at a table for one, a woman whose perfect dress and quiet manner suggested both charm and discretion.

"Don't you think she's more like one?" Mrs. Engel asked in a whisper. "I mean she looks kind of secretive and *perfumed.*"

"I don't know anything about it," said Mr. Engel, returning to his *pasta.*

"But she's always alone," Mrs. Engel pursued, "and the other one is always with a man. You know—not just one man. Any man." She laughed in a way unfamiliar to Mr. Engel. "Oh, well, as Mrs. Amburt said, there's one on every boat."

The sophistication that had come into Mrs. Engel's voice Mr. Engel knew to be only an echo, but somehow it disturbed him.

"There's a Mrs. Amburt on every boat, too," he said.

"How do you mean?" asked Mrs. Engel.

"Gossip," said Mr. Engel. "Nothing else to think about." He finished his *pasta* and signaled the steward to remove his plate.

"I don't think it's just gossip," said Mrs. Engel. "They said she doesn't even try *not* to be with men. She never even *speaks* to any of the women on board."

Mr. Engel studied the platter of cold meats that the steward brought. "Do they ever speak to her?" he asked, as he chose roast beef.

"Speak to her?" said Mrs. Engel, as she took cold chicken. "Speak to her," she repeated thoughtfully, with a quite different emphasis.

When dinner was over that night she left Mr. Engel to the last chapter of *The Brothers Karamazov* and made her way to where a young woman was sitting in the main lounge, waiting for the bingo game to begin. It was still early and not many people had come up from the dining room, and she was alone, except for the small boy who drooped against her. Her blue lace dress was limp, but her hair spilled to her shoulders like a shower of crisp autumn leaves. Mrs. Engel stopped at her table. "May I sit here for just a minute?" she asked. The young woman looked up at her, her eyes wary.

"Help yourself," she said. Mrs. Engel smiled down at the heavy-lidded child. "He's a good little boy, isn't he?" she said.

"He's hell on wheels," said the young woman. "Aren't you, lover?" she said to the child, and drew him closer to her. "He misses his D.A.D.D.Y," she spelled out in a whisper.

Mrs. Engel sat down.

The next morning she took her phrase book to her deck chair again and exchanged greetings with Mrs. Amburt and

Miss Orpen, or Orken. What she had in mind might not materialize at once, she knew, but people on shipboard adhere more or less to a pattern in their days, and it was not long before the young woman came in sight, leading her little boy, and followed, this time, by a man in a checked sport jacket. She had tied a scarf over her head, concealing her flaming hair, but she still looked as though she had just been unchained from something.

Mrs. Engel sat up straight. "Good morning," she called out in a voice that she felt was unduly piercing, but which arrested the young woman in her passage. She stopped, and the child, and the man in the sport jacket, stopped with her.

"Good morning," Mrs. Engel repeated, less shrilly, but clearly enough to carry well. "How is your little boy this morning? Did he have a good long sleep?"

"Yeah," said his mother, "he sure did."

"That's wonderful," said Mrs. Engel. "It doesn't hurt a child a bit to stay up late if he can make it up the next morning. And it's for such a short time," she hurried on, aware of the rigidity of Mrs. Amburt and Miss Orpen. "As soon as you rejoin your husband he can go back to his regular routine. It's such a shame that he missed his father so much when he had to leave. I mean, so that he never wanted you out of his sight, poor little boy. I expect he felt that if you left him, *you* might not come back, either."

"That's right," said the girl, "that's what the doctor told me." She moved as if to go, but Mrs. Engel detained her quickly. "Imagine!" she said, still in a rather high voice. "So that ever since your husband was sent abroad, you haven't been out of your son's sight!"

"He yelled if I left him," said the young woman simply.

"So you have to keep him with you every minute?" asked Mrs. Engel, feeling like a prompter in a quiz show.

"Well, sure," the girl answered. "You can't leave a kid to scream." Mrs. Engel played her last card. "But he'll be all right when he's with his father again, won't he?" she said.

"There'll be no holding him," said the young woman. "Me neither!" she added with a sudden surge. "Well, wonderful," said Mrs. Engel hastily, as Mrs. Amburt gasped.

The young woman ran her hand over the small head that was thrust against her, and loosened the small hands that clung to her. "O.K., kiddo," she said, "we got to get our exercise. Be seeing you," she said to Mrs. Engel, and as she started away Mrs. Engel thought she looked like a banner flying.

Mrs. Engel put on her glasses and settled back with her phrase book. "Her husband is doing some sort of information thing for the Army, one of those things with initials. He's been going to lots of places, but now he's going to be in *one* place, and they're sending her over to join him," she said to

Mrs. Amburt, casually. "I expect *that's* how she's traveling first class, don't you?"

"And that's how I did it," Mrs. Engel told Mr. Engel, at lunch.

"I don't see why you didn't just tell them quietly, the way you told me last night," said Mr. Engel.

"They wouldn't have told anyone else," said Mrs. Engel. "This way everyone around us heard. 'One on every boat'!" she quoted disdainfully. "She's a perfectly nice woman and she's *devoted* to her little boy."

"You told me," said Mr. Engel, sprinkling grated cheese on his asparagus.

"Of course, I suppose she *could* put him to bed early and stay down in the cabin with him at night, but do you know what I think?"

"No," said Mr. Engel.

"I think she's had no life at all since her husband left, and she's starved for it. She didn't *say* anything, but she kept looking at everything as if she were *hungry* for it. And she isn't brazen, the way they said. She is just friendly, and I'm going to be friendly back, and I'm going to say good morning to her every time I see her."

"Well, fine," said Mr. Engel.

"And I'll tell you something else," said Mrs. Engel. "I'm never again going to listen to what people say about other people, unless I know about them. It's awful to judge people by the way they look."

"Want dessert?" Mr. Engel asked.

"No, dear," said Mrs. Engel, "just tea."

When the tea came she sipped it slowly. "There's that woman just come in," she said.

"What woman?" asked Mr. Engel.

"The one with the green earrings, all by herself again."

"Isn't she always?" said Mr. Engel, more as a statement than a question.

"Yes," said Mrs. Engel, "and I think there's something funny about it. Do you know what I think? I think she's some kind of a spy or something, all mysterious like that, and always alone."

"What would she be spying on?" Mr. Engel asked mildly.

"I don't know," said Mrs. Engel darkly, "but if she isn't a spy, she's *something*."

Mr. Engel refilled his water glass. "She's an archaeologist," he said.

Mrs. Engel stared at him. "How do you know?" she asked.

"I knew you'd be wondering, so I asked the purser."

Mrs. Engel stared at Mr. Engel again, and then over his shoulder at the woman whose mystery was now gone.

"You mean, she's one of those people who dig things *up*?" she said incredulously.

"She's joining an excavation party in Sicily," said Mr. Engel.

Mrs. Engel said nothing more, but her husband thought that she took a long time to finish her one cup of tea.

When they had left the dining room and were waiting for the elevator, she spoke.

"I guess this boat is more than a dress rehearsal for Italy. It's a dress rehearsal for everything that we're going to see that we don't know about."

"Oh?" said Mr. Engel.

"I mean, we mustn't just look at something and say that's what it is, because it might be something else."

"You mean the Colosseum might be the Forum?" asked Mr. Engel, picking up Mrs. Engel's bag, which she had dropped.

She took it from him and shook her head.

"I don't mean monuments," she said. "I mean the people we'll see, and the way they live."

"Oh, well, sure," said Mr. Engel.

"All this gossip and everything has made me see *that*."

"Well, sure," said Mr. Engel again.

The elevator came, and when it had delivered the Engels to the sun deck, they settled at one of the umbrella-shaded tables that were set out there in calm weather. Mr. Engel produced a fresh paperback from his pocket, this time *Crime and*

Punishment, but Mrs. Engel just sat, looking out over the sunlit water to the horizon.

"Just the same," she said suddenly, "I can't see that woman digging!"

Mr. Engel looked at her, and her cheeks grew pink. She put a hand on his sleeve. "Well, there you are," she said, "that's *exactly* what I mean I mustn't do."

Mr. Engel went back to his book, but half absently he covered Mrs. Engel's hand with his own. When he withdrew it to turn a page, Mrs. Engel looked out to the horizon again and tried to see beyond it to all the things that were waiting for her. All the things that she would try to learn about, and try not to misunderstand. Thinking of them, all at once she found herself wishing that the ship would go faster.

LOOK LADY

*T*he roads to Rome are varied, and, while eventually the Engels were to take more than one of them, it was unfortunate that their first had been by way of Naples. In one brief stroll in that anomalous seaport Mr. Engel had been offered a dubious camera, a worthless fountain pen, a spurious wrist-watch, a packet of somewhat unorthodox postcards, and some-body's sister. He arrived, therefore, in the Eternal City, with an uneasy wariness of all things Italian and an instantaneous distrust of any suggestion made to him by anyone other than his wife and the Roman hotel porter, on whom he came to lean as on a brother. In fact, Mr. Engel felt on safer ground with the porter than with his wife, whose approach to the un-familiar was fearless. She was as innocent as she was enthusi-astic, he believed, and while he hesitated to tamper with either quality, he felt that combined they invited trouble, so from time to time he ventured mild warnings which Mrs. Engel brushed aside.

"Just because they offered you those postcards in Naples you're suspicious of everything," she said one day. They were having tea in the chandeliered lounge of their hotel, and she had borrowed Mr. Engel's pen to address some postcards of her own which she had spread on their tea table. "There's been nothing like that here in Rome," she went on, "just that little man with the cameos and they were all right. Well, they weren't genuine, but they were perfectly *nice*."

Mr. Engel blushed. "I wouldn't have told you about the postcards," he said, "except that I wanted you to be careful."

"They wouldn't offer things like that to a woman," said

Mrs. Engel, putting Mr. Engel's pen on her plate while she refilled her cup, "so I don't see what I'm to be careful of."

Mr. Engel removed his pen to a plate that had no crumbs on it. "That's what I'm trying to tell you," he said patiently. "It isn't only the postcards. I don't think you ought to rush at people here the way you do."

Mrs. Engel put down her cup. "Who do I rush at?" she asked.

"Everyone. And these Italians are funny about women, they might—well, they might misunderstand you."

Mrs. Engel looked interested rather than impressed. "At my age? What would they do?"

"How would *I* know," said Mr. Engel hastily, but some of the insinuations of the insistent men in Naples came back to him, and he blushed again. How to enlighten Mrs. Engel, however, was beyond him, and he merely repeated that she ought to be more cautious.

"Well, I'll try," she said doubtfully, "but I think it's silly." She went back to addressing her postcards, and Mr. Engel moved the cream pitcher out of range of her elbow. "The thing is," she said, while continuing to write, "even if you'd bought those postcards, they'd probably have turned out to be just views of Paris. They substitute them. Well, that's what they *do*," she repeated in answer to Mr. Engel's look of astonishment. "Didn't you know that? And the other things like the watches with no works, they don't mean to be dishonest about them, it's just that they're so poor, and they think we're so rich." She made a cross on the front of a postcard that showed part of their hotel. "The thing is," she said then, "I don't want to miss anything, and if I'm cautious all the time, I might. For instance, if I had been cautious with Look Lady I would have missed all sorts of things."

"Look Lady?" asked Mr. Engel.

"Aquillino, our taxi driver. That's what he says all the time—'look, lady'—and every time he says it you jump, and every time he wants to show us something that isn't a church you go all stiff. You're even suspicious of *him*."

"No I'm not," said Mr. Engel.

"Yes, you are," said Mrs. Engel, "and whenever I ask him to show us something different, something that isn't just a monument, you turn green."

"I do not," said Mr. Engel. "I just don't know where he'll take us."

"But that's what's fun," said Mrs. Engel, "and he knows places the other taximen don't know. Like the very first day we had him, even the porter didn't know where that restaurant was, but Aquillino did."

The restaurant had been recommended to Mrs. Engel by a friend, who had remembered everything about it except its name.

"It has wisteria all over it, and it's up a lot of steps from the roadside, and it's on the Appian Way," Mrs. Engel had told the hotel doorman, "so will you please explain to the driver, *per favore.*" The driver had been Aquillino, summoned from the taxi stand at the top of the Via Sistina. He had listened carefully to the doorman, and then had beamed.

"*H'oh*kay," he said, and when they were in his cab he spoke again. "Very good place, very pretty outside, very near Catacombs. I get you there *subito.*"

"You speak English!" Mrs. Engel exclaimed, "what does *subito* mean?"

"Very quick, nice and fast," said Aquillino.

"Well, then," said Mrs. Engel, "not too *subito*, we like to go slow and see things."

Aquillino looked round at her in sudden joy, letting his cab take care of itself.

"Slow and see things," he cried, "is best way, is only way! I go slow now and show you everything."

"*Tante grazie!*" said Mrs. Engel.

"*Prego, signora,*" said Aquillino, and Mr. Engel had closed his eyes as the cab took itself through a cross street and a red light simultaneously.

Aquillino recovered control, and once they reached the Appian Way he slowed as he had promised. He stopped once to let Mrs. Engel walk on a segment of the original paving, and glowed over her awe. Driving on, he pointed out tombs and villas and gardens with catholic enthusiasm, and reaching the restaurant he told them the best thing to order. "Chicken all burned up," he explained happily, "put on leaves, set fire to leaves. *Molto buono*." He agreed to wait for them without argument, and after they had lunched he heartily supported Mrs. Engel's reluctance to visit the Catacombs.

"People dead," he said. "More nice to see people alive." He waved in illustration toward a young Italian speeding by on a motorcycle, a girl seated sidesaddle behind him, her starched skirts tucked neatly against the wind, as serenely feminine as a Gibson girl in a canoe.

On the way back he answered Mrs. Engel's questions in a splendid jumble of English and Italian incomprehensible to Mr. Engel, but from which Mrs. Engel learned that for generations Aquillino's family had driven and guided visitors through Rome. Rome was their pride, and Aquillino was as anxious to exhibit his city as Mrs. Engel was to know it. From then on he was her own. Daily she took him from wherever he stood in his taxi rank, until his companions, ordinarily ferocious in the matter of precedence, became resigned and simply shrugged to each other when Mrs. Engel disregarded it.

At first Aquillino only took the Engels where they directed him, but gradually he began to suggest lesser landmarks on less beaten tracks.

He took them to a tiny square tucked away behind a greater one where a modest tower bore a clock emblazoned in gold, and the colors of a mosaic madonna triumphed over the centuries. He showed them markets that thrived in obscure streets where people lived as isolated from the city around them as if they lived on the moon. He produced new vistas with the air of a conjuror, and sometimes his relish of Mrs. Engel's response was so wholehearted that Mr. Engel would walk a little way off from them until they were restored to some measure of calm. Aquillino took them to the Punch and Judy show in the Pinchio gardens and breathed warmly down Mr. Engel's neck as he stood with them to watch it. He laughed in sympathy with Mrs. Engel's delight in the balloon sellers who drifted among the trees of the park, their wares clustered high at the ends of long sticks so that they rose in the sunlight like explosions of fireworks.

All simple things, all harmless things, Mr. Engel admitted, but he would have enjoyed them more if he had always known about them in advance. The element of mystery that Mrs. Engel welcomed and invited was only a source of added apprehension to him, like the night Aquillino had driven them to the Campidoglio. In spite of the floodlit monuments and buildings nearby, the approach seemed eerie, and the night oppressive.

"What's he up to?" Mr. Engel asked his wife.

"He wouldn't say," she answered, "he just asked if he could come and get us tonight. It's a surprise. He isn't going to *murder* us," she had added, as Mr. Engel clung tensely to the strap at his elbow. "He just wants to show us something."

"But we've been up here before," said Mr. Engel, "we've been here twice before. What's he bringing us here for *now?*"

Then the cab stopped and Aquillino got out. His smile under his clipped mustache was secret, and he opened the cab door with the effect of having his finger on his lips. He helped the Engels out and then stood a little apart from them. "Look, lady," he said and pointed up to the Palace that stood alone at the summit of the Campidoglio. Before, by daylight, it had been no more than another historic building, austere and impersonal, but now it was a fairy palace, intangible against the night sky, its façade iced with candles—slender false tapers—the very steadiness of their pointed, unflickering lights enhancing its look of unreality, of something dreamed.

"Look, lady!" said Aquillino again, and flung out his arms to the sight as if he had created it.

"It isn't lit like that very often," Mrs. Engel said as they drove back to the hotel, "and he was afraid we might not be here to see it again."

"But why couldn't he have told us what it was?" said Mr. Engel. "I mean *why* he was taking us up there?"

"It would have spoiled it," said Mrs. Engel, "you know it would."

Now she addressed a last postcard, and turned it over to look at its picture side again. "I might never have seen this if it hadn't been for Look Lady," she said. "All the other drivers take you to the Trevi, but Look Lady took us to the Tortoise Fountain because he loves it himself, and he thought I would. And I did. He does wonderful things for us, and when I try to speak Italian he doesn't look bored with me the way some of the shop people do, he's *delighted.*" Her voice took on the slight rise that Mr. Engel knew presaged tears. "He behaves as if we *belong* to him, and he makes everything seem as if it were there just for us."

"Just for you," said Mr. Engel, striving for lightness. "He always says 'look, lady,' he never says 'look, sir'!"

Mrs. Engel let her postcards run through her fingers. "Well, you don't always react much to things," she said carefully, "and then, I think he is a little afraid of you. I think he knows you don't really trust him." She took off her glasses and put them on the table and got up. "I'll take these down and get stamps for them," she said, picking up the postcards.

Mr. Engel signed the check, retrieved his fountain pen and Mrs. Engel's glasses from the plate where she had left them, and followed her to the porter's desk.

After that day he made an honest effort to stifle whatever qualms he might have. He restrained himself from checking each step with the porter, and tried to believe that Mrs. Engel was right, and that Aquillino would never misinterpret her enthusiasm. He followed Mrs. Engel and Aquillino docilely through dim and crumbling crypts, and descended with them to a churchly excavation where daylight was forgotten and the Tiber throbbed angrily beneath treacherous planking. He suffered them to take him into the Colosseum at night where he kept to himself the thought that even if Aquillino could be trusted, there was nothing to prevent all three of them being set on from the Stygian recesses behind them. Gradually, Naples faded, and Mr. Engel relaxed.

Then one afternoon Mrs. Engel engaged Aquillino to take them to the Protestant Cemetery, an expedition so normal that Mr. Engel looked forward to it. For once he knew where he was going, there was slight chance of sudden surprise, and they would be in daylight, and aboveground. He was almost cheerful, therefore, when they reached the Cemetery and left Aquillino to wait for them at its gate.

The Cemetery was green and still, and its tranquillity touched what sadness it held with comfort. It had rained earlier in the day, and under the soft grayness of the sky the trees and shrubs glistened over the gathered dead.

"But it doesn't seem final for them here the way it does in the crypts and tombs," Mrs. Engel whispered. "They're from so many places, it's as if they were just waiting to go home."

The Engels went slowly up and down the tiered paths and stood without speaking by the grave of Shelley. Then they went to where Keats lay under his own youthful, bitter epitaph.

"It's such a little grave," Mrs. Engel said, "like the room he died in. It was such a *little* room." She read the epitaph aloud, and then, with her hand in Mr. Engel's, walked with him out to the taxi.

Aquillino looked troubled when he saw her.

"It made you sad, lady," he said. "You like now I take you someplace nice? Someplace funny?"

"Oh, yes, Aquillino," Mrs. Engel said, as she got into the cab with Mr. Engel, "I'd love to see something nice and funny."

His smile widening to show the two china-white synthetic teeth that made him look like a friendly squirrel, Aquillino bore them off. The sun had come out again and Rome was responding with a richer gold. They passed the Baths of Caracalla and went on along a rising road, and then up a shorter, steeper one. They passed a convent, Mrs. Engel thought, or an orphanage, and then a church and monastery, flanked by a modest park where old and young people strolled, and nuns scurried after children that ran laughing through

the trees. There were bright flower beds in the park and the
sunset was sending long red fingers to touch the green about
them with a hint of autumn. Mrs. Engel exclaimed with pleasure, but Aquillino carried them on to a square, open and high-
walled, and at this hour deserted. Here he stopped and got
out. "Look, lady," he said as he opened the cab door, "now
you see something funny."

Mrs. Engel looked out from the cab. "I don't see *anything*," she said.

Aquillino writhed coyly. "Is secret," he said. "Very funny,
very *singolare*. The *signora* must come peep."

Mrs. Engel started to get out, but Mr. Engel put a hand
on her arm. "Wait a minute," he said. "What did he say just
now?"

"*Singolare*," she said. "I think it means singular, or strange
or something."

"No, he said something else. He said you would have to do
something."

"Oh," said Mrs. Engel, "he said I'd have to peep. Like
round a corner or through something, I suppose."

"Peep at *what?*" asked Mr. Engel.

"Why, I don't know," said his wife.

"Ask him," said Mr. Engel.

Mrs. Engel looked at him, and then at Aquillino who was
still waiting, puzzled.

"The *signore* wants to know what it is?" she said to him.

Aquillino squirmed. "Please, lady, is a surprise. I tell—then no surprise. Please, you come."

But Mr. Engel sat still, his hand on Mrs. Engel's arm, and Aquillino gave in.

"Is keyhole," he said, "peep in keyhole, very funny, very *curiosa.*"

"Very what?" Mr. Engel asked his wife.

"Very curious," she said lightly, and saw Mr. Engel freeze.

"I told you something like this would happen," he said under his breath. "Well, you're not going to look through any keyhole. Tell him to take us home."

"Oh," said Mrs. Engel, after a moment. "You're thinking of Naples again. The postcards and everything."

Mr. Engel did not reply to this. "Just tell him the hotel," he repeated.

"Hotel?" asked Aquillino, who had caught the word. "We go back?"

"No, wait," said Mrs. Engel, "*una momento.*" She turned to Mr. Engel. "Will you look *first?*" she said, and before he could reply she turned once more to the puzzled Aquillino. "*Prego,* let the *signore* look first. Please, dear," she said to her husband, "get out and look first." She sat back and waited.

Reluctantly Mr. Engel got out of the cab. He stood looking down at Aquillino, and all Naples had come back to him.

When he spoke it was awkwardly, but disgust sharpened and colored his voice, and he looked, Mrs. Engel thought, as if he had seen a snake.

"All right," he said, "where is this—this keyhole?"

In themselves the words were nothing, but the tone of them carried a meaning to Aquillino, and a slow comprehension began in his face. Beside Mr. Engel he looked very small, Mrs. Engel thought, and he seemed to be asking a question without hope of understanding the answer. A spot of red came in his cheeks, and he made an odd gesture, half-disclaimer, half-withdrawal. Then he walked across the square and stopped at a wooden door. Mr. Engel joined him, and Aquillino indicated a round hole cut in the door at about the place where a keyhole would be. Then he stood aside.

Mr. Engel bent and looked into the opening for a moment, then he straightened and signaled to Mrs. Engel. She came without hurrying, and bent to the keyhole in her turn. Set in its circle she saw a long line of tiny trees, their branches meeting to make a minute green arch, and at its very end the dome of St. Peter's was centered against a spangle of sun, reduced, as was the whole scene, by some trick of perspective to a miniature. It was like a view from a doll's house, she thought, or as if a memory of it had become a pinprick in someone's mind.

6

53

She stood erect and spoke to Aquillino slowly and carefully so that he would understand her.

"The *signore* wished to look first because he thought it was a thing to frighten me. Like the Catacombs. You know how frightened I was of the Catacombs. I wouldn't even go in."

Aquillino nodded, but kept his eyes on the ground.

"But this was beautiful," she said. "Not *curious*, beautiful. *Bellissima. Tante grazie.*"

"*Prego, signora,*" he said quietly, and led the way back to his cab.

"You see," said Mrs. Engel gently as they rode homeward. "By curious he just meant unusual. It's like me not knowing the right words in Italian." Then, as Mr. Engel did not answer, she said no more.

For the next day or two Aquillino was absent from his place in the taxi rank, but finally Mrs. Engel caught sight of him and hailed him. He seemed reluctant to respond, and when he did he avoided meeting Mr. Engel's eye.

"Someplace different," Mrs. Engel told him, and Mr. Engel thought it sounded more like a plea than an order, "something we haven't seen before."

Aquillino hesitated, but obedience was strong in him, and submissively he turned his cab and set off. Presently he drew up at an unfamiliar building. He led them through the main courtyard, and then through a second, neglected and unswept. Dust and paper blew around Mrs. Engel's feet. "Is *h'oh*kay, lady," said Aquillino, "is better in next one." His voice sounded dull, Mr. Engel thought, as though something had been rubbed off.

The third courtyard was unpaved. It might once have been a garden but now there was only bare earth. In its center stood a tunnel, open at both ends, like an outsized relic of a toy railway.

"Look, lady," said Aquillino, and Mr. Engel went with his wife to the tunnel's entrance.

It was another conceit in perspective, painted and graded to suggest height and length, perhaps conceived originally as a conversation piece, a delicate joke. To emphasize the illusion, just outside its exit was a graceful statue, debatable as to size.

"Look, lady," said Aquillino, his voice still dull, "is big statue, or is little statue?"

Mrs. Engel laughed, and Mr. Engel cleared his throat.

"It's a big statue," he said, before Mrs. Engel could answer.

Aquillino turned to him. "Big?" he asked. "Statue is *very* big?"

Mr. Engel looked into space. "Very big," he said.

Life came back to Aquillino. His mustache bristling, his

teeth shining, he led the Engels through the few feet of tunnel
to the statue at its end.

"Is little," he crowed, patting it on the head, "is a trick!"

He took the Engels back to his cab and stowed them inside
it, then he addressed Mr. Engel directly.

"Was a good trick?" he asked, and it was as if he had put
out his hand.

"It was fine," said Mr. Engel, as if he were taking it.

A little later they passed the Tortoise Fountain, its four
male figures reaching to push four tortoises to the gushing
waters of its basin. Aquillino turned joyfully from his wheel.
"Look, lady," he cried. *"Look*, gentleman——"

A moment after the Engels left the jeweler's shop on the Via Condotti, Mrs. Engel opened the box she was carrying and extracted the silver charm bracelet she had just bought. "I love it," she said, dangling it in the light. "I simply love it."

She dropped the bracelet in the box, and continued with Mr. Engel toward the Spanish Steps.

In the middle of a crossing she stopped, and Mr. Engel had to push her forward out of the path of a shrieking phalanx of motorcycles. "What's the matter?" he asked.

"I've just realized!" she answered. "Do you know what I said to the man?"

"What man?"

"The jeweler. I told him I loved him! That's actually what I said. I meant I loved the bracelet, but I got the pronoun wrong and I should have said *'piacere,'* not *'amo.'* 'It pleases me'—that's what I should have said. Oh, well, he probably knew what I meant."

Mr. Engel considered this. Whether the jeweler understood or misunderstood Mrs. Engel's intention was not important; what was important was his own wish that she wouldn't keep on trying to speak Italian when it wasn't necessary. On their recent trip to the hill towns, her limited knowledge had often been useful, but now they were back in Rome, where almost everyone they had contact with understood English, and he wished that Mrs. Engel could somehow be brought to believe it. He had a theory about speaking Italian and was about to enlarge on it, but they had reached the Spanish Steps, and the ascent, slowly though they went, took all his breath. He would have preferred a taxi, but Mrs. Engel liked the

Steps, with their burden of people. Sometimes she spoke to one or another of them, and always she waved to the babies, with the inverted Italian wave that she had adopted. After they had gained the top, he stood with her, watching the city below turn to apricot in the waning sunlight, then steered her back to their hotel nearby, to sink thankfully into the white-painted chairs in the courtyard, where they always had their cocktail. It was early evening; the swifts were making dusky circles in the deepening sky, and the flowers on the hotel terrace were as brilliant as stained glass. Mrs. Engel surveyed the scene happily.

"Bello," she murmured. *"Molto bello."*

Mr. Engel sighed. "Another?" He indicated her glass.

"What time is it?" she asked.

"About seven-thirty."

"No, then," she said. "I'll wait till before dinner."

Mr. Engel held up a finger to the darkly handsome young man who was in suave charge of the semicircular, gaily awninged bar. "Check, please."

"You should say *'il conto,'*" said Mrs. Engel dreamily. " 'Bill' in England, *'l'addition'* in France, *'il conto'* in Italy."

"Check," Mr. Engel repeated, and almost at once it was at his fingers. He had signed it, noted the service charge, and added a few more lire than were recommended by the book on "How to Tip and Travel in Europe," which was as much a companion to him as the phrase books and dictionaries that made Mrs. Engel's packing a problem were to her. He collected her glasses, gloves, bag, and wrap, and moved with her to the elevator.

"I don't see why you won't," she said, as he pressed the button.

"Won't what?"

"You know perfectly well what. All this time here, and you won't even try. It's just as easy to say *'conto'* as 'check.' *'Conto'* is what you say."

"Not what I say," he replied when the elevator came and, as always, he had to pull Mrs. Engel back from the door, which treacherously opened outward.

After they had got in and she had said, "*Settimo piano, per favore,*" and the boy had said, "Seven' floor, *h'oh*kay," no one said anything more.

"Want to have dinner here or out?" Mr. Engel asked, as he unlocked their door and let his wife pass in. "Whichever you like," she answered, going to the long windows and opening them to the narrow balcony.

"Well, I'd like to go back to that place by the fountain where they have the ravioli."

There are many fountains in Rome, and there is ravioli in every restaurant adjacent to them. Mrs. Engel turned on him. "You see! You won't even say an Italian *name*. You could mean anywhere. No one would know *where* you meant!"

"Well, *you* know," he replied placidly. "Want to go there?"

"Yes," she said. She took a black taffeta dress from the wardrobe, spread it on her bed, and began trying the effect of an artificial pink camellia on one shoulder. Then she returned to the attack. "I don't understand you," she said. "Italian is so easy; you don't even have to pronounce it. *'Conto,'* that's all you have to say—*'conn-to.'*" She drew it out a little.

Mr. Engel went to the table that he used as a bureau, and began putting all the things from his pockets on it. Then he removed his coat and vest, and hung them over a chair.

"You won't even try," his wife went on. "I wish you would just *try*."

Mr. Engel took off his tie. "What do you want me to do?" he asked. "Go around telling jewelers that I love them?"

"That isn't fair!" said Mrs. Engel hotly. "Just because I made a mistake and told you! I suppose now you'll think *everything* I say is wrong!"

"No," said Mr. Engel, "though I don't think it's always right—like this 'chow' thing you say."

"*What* 'chow thing'?"

"You say it all the time. Every time you see a child, you rush at it and say 'Chow.'"

"Oh," said Mrs. Engel. "You mean *'Ciao.'*"

"That's what I said—'chow.' Well, I asked the porter about that; I asked him what *is* this 'chow,' and he told me it's something Italian people say like a greeting——"

"I know it is," Mrs. Engel interrupted. "It's like 'Hi' or 'Hello, there.'"

Mr. Engel shook his head. "It's a little more than that. It's something Italian people say to other Italian people, and then only if they know them very well. It's a familiar sort of thing, but you say it to people you don't even know."

"I only say it to children—it's all right to say it to *children*."

Mr. Engel got out his dark-blue suit and looked around for his clothesbrush. "But why do you say it to *them*? You don't rush at strange children at home and say 'Hi' to them."

"I don't do lots of things at home. I don't sleep in the afternoon at home; I don't have a cocktail before dinner and then before dinner *again*; I don't have dinner at ten o'clock at night at home."

Mr. Engel found his clothesbrush and began using it. "Neither do I," he said. "But that doesn't make me talk to strangers."

Just then, the telephone rang. Mrs. Engel answered it, saying *"Pronto"* with just enough authority to provoke a flood of Italian, which had to be stemmed and diverted into English on both sides.

Mr. Engel listened as his wife took down a message from one of the shops, translated by the operator. "Look," he said when it was done. "That's really what I mean. It isn't your getting it wrong—anyone can do that. It's using it when you don't need to, and making them think you speak their language when you don't. You say a word like that one, and they come back at you with a stream of stuff that you can't understand a word of, while if you said 'Hello' in the first place, they'd speak English right off. I just feel you confuse them."

"They don't all speak English," said Mrs. Engel reasonably. "Sometimes I *have* to speak Italian. I got you that extra blanket that cold night in Assisi," she reminded him, "and sometimes I have to ask the way to places."

"Do you understand what they answer?"

"They always point," said Mrs. Engel, "but they wouldn't if I wasn't able to *ask*."

Mr. Engel conceded the truth of this, but it still wasn't what he meant. When Italian was necessary, he said, it was fine to know a little, and right to use it. What he really meant was that Mrs. Engel shouldn't give the impression of being able to converse in Italian.

"Oh, I think they know I can't," she said.

"Then why do you do it?"

MR. AND MRS. ENGEL
Chowl 64

Mrs. Engel fingered the camellia, which she had pinned on her dress. "I like to communicate," she said slowly. "I like to try to reach them. When I talk to the children, for instance, it's more for their parents—they're so proud of them, and mostly they're the only things they *have*. So even if I say it all wrong, they'll know I'm trying to reach them, and then maybe they'll try to reach *me*." She hesitated a moment. "It's being friendly—and it's fun," she finished, rather lamely.

Mr. Engel took a clean shirt and went to wash. When he came back his wife was sitting at the dressing table, doing something to her hair. He dressed and began putting all the things from the table back into his pockets. "Listen," he said. "I'm not criticizing you. I only feel that when they understand English, you should stick to it. I think it's more sensible that way, at least till you can keep Italian *up*. Can't you be friendly in English?"

Mrs. Engel stepped into her dress and backed up to him to have it zipped. "Just start it for me," she said, "so it won't stick."

He pulled it halfway up. "You see what I mean?" he asked. "I think the other way sounds silly."

Mrs. Engel faced him. "You mean *I* sound silly?"

Mr. Engel took a moment or two to answer her. "Not you especially," he said then, carefully. "Anyone."

"I see what you mean," she said, and went and stood in

front of the wardrobe mirror but without actually looking at herself in it. "Of course I see."

"I'm not criticizing," Mr. Engel said again.

"I know," said his wife.

"Well, ready?" he asked, as she still stood there.

"Go ahead. You go ahead. I'll be right down."

He looked at her uneasily, but she smiled reassuringly. "Go ahead, dear," she said. "I just have to get my other bag."

He went into the hall and rang for the elevator, but it was slow, and she was beside him before it came. She was carrying her evening bag and a light fur stole. She had taken off the pink camellia.

She said nothing as they rode down, just smiling when the boy said good evening, and when they reached the lobby she remained silent. Ordinarily, she took over the taxi situation, first exchanging *Buona seras* with the doorman, then explaining their destination, which he transmitted to the driver, Mrs. Engel repeating the direction and adding, when they started off, "*Ma non troppo presto, per favore,*" although she always leaned forward in her seat as if pushing on to an adventure. That night, she left it all to Mr. Engel, and, once in the cab, she just settled back.

At the restaurant, it was the same; she bowed to the head-waiter's ebullient greeting as he led them to one of the choice pavement tables, separated from the street only by a plant-lined railing, low enough to give them a view of the great square, which was really a long rectangle. They could see the fountain, its immense figures writhing below a darkened church, and the people sitting out on the benches, and the inevitable children running and swirling in and out of the shadows like night moths. Mr. Engel handed her the menu and waited for her to translate for him after consultation with the waiter, but she handed it back to him and said, "I'd like the casserole, and the asparagus—and the ravioli first, of course."

The waiter remembered them. On their first visit, Mrs. Engel had explained that they couldn't eat a whole portion of ravioli apiece. *"Non posso,"* she had said. *"Appetito americano, non italiano."* The waiter had laughed, then, and he laughed now as he reminded her of it, but Mrs. Engel merely nodded. "Yes," she said. "One portion for two."

The waiter bowed, quickly correct again, but she seemed not to notice. She removed her gloves and laid them carefully on the table beside her plate, looking at nothing in particular.

Mr. Engel studied her. Was she angry with him after all, he wondered. Was she giving him the silent treatment? He knew all her silences; he knew when she was happily silent, when she was broodingly silent, and when she was harboringly silent, but this, somehow, was none of them.

Their Martinis came, and they sipped them; she met his eyes across them calmly, and there was no rancor in her gaze. He was relieved. She wasn't hurt or angry. Perhaps she was tired, although she didn't look it. She looked more the way she did at home after a club meeting or an afternoon's bridge—not tired, but quiet.

She was being sensible about it, he decided, the way he had explained she should be. The waiter understood English, so she was speaking English, and that was all there was to it. Just the same, there was something wrong. He cast around for conversation. "This is a good place," he said. "I'm glad we came back to Rome."

"It's very pleasant," she said.

"That's right," he said, and immediately realized that it was all wrong; "pleasant" was not a word she had ever used about Rome. It wasn't a word for Rome anyway, he thought. You could call it lots of things, depending on how it struck you—gaudy, tawdry, battered, dirty, noisy. Or—he groped for unaccustomed adjectives—colorful, maybe, or romantic, but never pleasant. "Pleasant" meant someplace clean and bright and impersonal, yet that was what she had said, and she seemed to mean it and be satisfied with it.

They ate the ravioli and the casserole, and endured the vagrant musicians who came to stand near them in the street outside—the blind guitarist with his weary dog, and his female accomplice, who held a hopeless saucer over the railing toward them.

Mr. Engel put some change into it.

"At least, they don't come and play at you over the table," he said. He and Mrs. Engel shared a violent distaste for restaurant violinists who yearned at you. "Right into your *soup*," she had often said.

"No, they don't," she agreed now, without any answering spark.

That was it, thought Mr. Engel; she had no spark. It was as if a lamp had been turned off somewhere in a room; the room wasn't exactly dimmer, you could still see everything, yet you missed something. He looked out at the square, rich in history, dark with the past, lit now with the present. Voices reached him. The warm night was heavy with them: the voices of mothers and children and of young men who were playing some kind of violent but hilarious game; voices of tourists, Americans like himself, strolling about, only half aware of what they were seeing or where they were. That was it, he thought—only half aware. And vaguely it came to him what Mrs. Engel had been trying for. To understand, maybe—to get a little closer to this incomprehensible city. She had been reaching out to it, eagerly aware, and now she sat across from him as she might anywhere—in Scarsdale, he thought, or Bronxville—but this was Rome. The name rolled out in his mind and became a limitless scroll, and it seemed to have Mrs. Engel's name written along its entire length. She had had joy in the very idea of Rome, and he had cut it off; he had subdued her. *That* was the right word. She wasn't quiet; she was subdued, and he knew now that the last thing he wanted was a subdued Mrs. Engel.

It was time to ask for the check. He signaled to the waiter and took a long breath. *"Conto,"* he said, a little more loudly than he had meant to. *"Il conto."*

He didn't look at Mrs. Engel, though he felt her sudden look toward him. He counted his change carefully and distributed indiscriminate tips. He collected Mrs. Engel's gloves, bag, glasses, and stole, and walked out to the square with her. They found a bench and sat down. Beside them sat a shapeless woman with a little girl in her arms who had the fragile, pale face of a primitive painting.

Mrs. Engel leaned to her. *"Bella,"* she said. *"Bellissima."*

The woman's face illuminated, and she held the child high for them to admire. Mrs. Engel laughed and made the inverted wave. *"Ciao,"* she said, and turned at last to Mr. Engel. Her eyes were alive again, and expectant.

Mr. Engel swallowed, and waved to the child in his own way. "Chow!" he said, and he felt Mrs. Engel's arm slip through his.

*A*lthough Mrs. Engel was not a Catholic, she felt that to be in Rome and not see the Pope was to miss something essential. It was like eating an artichoke and ignoring the heart, she thought, but she had no practical idea how to rectify it. She was aware that the Pope gave a daily benediction from his window overlooking St. Peter's Square, but she and her husband had never been there at the right hour, which was approximately noon. The thing to do was to plan for it and go, she knew, but she was shy about suggesting it, for while she was an Episcopalian, Mr. Engel was a Congregationalist, when he remembered it, and she was not sure how he would take to being publicly blessed. She would go alone some morning when he was having his hair cut, or something, she promised herself, and then, one afternoon, she ran into Miss Murphy.

Half an hour later, she burst in on Mr. Engel, who was sitting on his bed with a number of lira notes spread around him. "What do you think?" she demanded, her eyes shining.

"I know one thing I think," Mr. Engel replied. "Something ought to be done about these ten-thousand-lira notes. No one will change them, and I've got to have something to tip with."

"I know, it's a shame, but who do you think I met buying postcards from the porter?" said his wife, in one breath. "Do you remember Miss Murphy?"

"No," said Mr. Engel.

"Yes, you do. She was on the boat with us coming over. She wore that suit with the funny pockets, and she has a sister who's a nun. Don't you remember her? You danced with her once."

"I never danced with a nun," said Mr. Engel definitely.

"I meant with Miss *Murphy,* the time they had that change-partners waltz. *She* remembers it. She spoke of it twice. Well, anyway, that's who she is, and she's staying right here in the hotel—and where do you think she's taking me?"

"I don't know," said Mr. Engel. "Waltzing?"

"No," said Mrs. Engel. "I *wish* you wouldn't spoil things."

Mr. Engel relented. "Where, then?" he asked, gathering his money together.

"Well," said Mrs. Engel, "she's taking me to an audience." Mr. Engel looked vague. "The *Pope.* She's taking me to see the Pope."

"Oh," said Mr. Engel.

"I can't *believe* it," his wife went on. "It won't be like seeing him from the Square, the way anyone can. This is *indoors.*" She paused. "Not indoors in his apartments. That's only for very small groups. This one is for several groups combined, so it's sort of biggish. It's to be in St. Peter's."

"The church?"

"The Basilica," Mrs. Engel amended.

"That's more than sort of biggish, that's big. How will you be able to see him there?"

Mrs. Engel glowed. "Miss Murphy has tickets for places

in a special stand, like a royal box, or something—I suppose because her sister's a nun. The tickets are a special color. Wasn't it wonderful that she had two? She was going to return one when she met *me*."

"When is it to be?"

"Tomorrow, at noon, but we're going to get there at eleven, because they don't reserve the seats in the box, and we want to be right in front." She beamed at Mr. Engel. "Aren't you excited?"

"Excited?"

"Well, *interested*, then."

"I suppose so," said Mr. Engel, putting his money in his wallet.

Mrs. Engel hesitated. "Do you—do you *mind* my going?" she asked tentatively.

"I don't mind," her husband answered. "I just thought you didn't like crowds."

"We have *seats*," Mrs. Engel said. "We even go in by a private entrance. This isn't a *crowd*—this is an *audience*." She let the word linger, and then went to her wardrobe and surveyed her dresses. "*Now* the thing is, what am I going to wear? Of course, *she's* going to wear black with a mantilla, the way they do, but I don't think I should. . . . Anyway, I haven't got a mantilla," she added, a little wistfully.

"I don't see why you have to dress up for it," said Mr. Engel.

Before Mrs. Engel answered this, she somehow managed to give the impression that she had counted up to ten. "It wouldn't be dressing up if I wore a mantilla. It would be manners—like wearing three feathers when you're presented at court." She pushed her dresses along the hanger rail. "My black is too cocktaily. Do you think my navy blue would do, with my black hat, if I took the flowers off?"

Mr. Engel had collected a dacron shirt and a box of soap flakes, which he shook experimentally. "Remind me to get some more of these," he said, and retired to the bathroom.

Mrs. Engel examined her black hat. Without its trimming, it would be no more than a head covering, but, after all, that was the idea, she supposed. She had one brief vision of herself correct and remote in the mystery of drifting black lace, and dismissed it. Mantillas and Mr. Engel would not mix, she decided. But before she reached for her scissors, she telephoned an order to the porter. If a mantilla was beyond her, the hotel car service was not, and the deference of a limousine she could, and would, contribute.

The next morning, at ten-thirty, Mr. Engel helped Miss Murphy into the symbolic limousine and asked his invariable questions of Mrs. Engel. "Have you got everything? Bag, money, glasses?"

Mrs. Engel, whose mouth was oddly dry, nodded.

"Medals," said Miss Murphy. "Have you your medals?"

Mrs. Engel looked bewildered. "Medals?" She thought of Mr. Engel's Purple Heart. "I'm afraid not. Not *with* me."

"Ah, that's too bad," said Miss Murphy. "Any religious article you carry or wear will get the blessing." She indicated a small parcel tucked under her arm. "Rosaries and medals to take home."

"Oh," said Mrs. Engel. "You mean *saints!* I have a St. Christopher medal"—Miss Murphy smiled tolerantly—"but it's on the car at home. Oh dear, I would so love to have a *blessed* St. Christopher." She looked wildly down the street toward the shops. "I suppose there isn't time to——"

"There isn't," said Mr. Engel, "and you're blocking the taxis."

Mrs. Engel looked at him imploringly. "If only I had thought of it in time," she said.

"You'll be late," said Mr. Engel. He urged her in, nodded to the chauffeur, and stood, half waving, as the car started away.

"He's a fine-looking man," said Miss Murphy, "and a grand waltzer. He didn't remember me, though: he didn't know me from Adam."

Mrs. Engel wrenched herself from St. Christopher. "It was your mantilla," she invented hastily. "He's more used to you in a hat." She gave a side glance at Miss Murphy. Remembering some of her less fortunate shipboard costumes, Mrs. Engel thought that the Pope's ruling on dress had much to be said for it. It was not only modest, it was helpful. Miss Murphy looked actually distinguished, Mrs. Engel acknowledged—and wished she could think the same of herself. The denuded hat, softened with a veil ripped from another hat, looked better than she had hoped, and her dark dress was simple, but the total effect, she was afraid, was no more than unobtrusive.

"I would have worn a mantilla, too," she told Miss Murphy, "but I wasn't sure that I *should*."

"It isn't obligatory, it isn't obligatory at all," Miss Murphy assured her, just touching her own black lace. "The Holy Father has relaxed the rule considerably. Of course, this is a public audience. A private one would be another matter altogether."

"Have you been to one like that?" asked Mrs. Engel.

"I've not been to one of any kind," said Miss Murphy, "but there's established procedure for all."

"Is it difficult?" asked Mrs. Engel, seeing herself backing out of St. Peter's. "Will I be able to do it properly?"

"You'll not have to do anything," said Miss Murphy. "Just sit in your place and don't stir till we kneel for the blessing."

"But when the Pope—when the Holy *Father*—comes in,"
said Mrs. Engel, "don't we do anything then?"

"Well, he won't *come* in, he'll be carried in on his chair,"
Miss Murphy said. "It may be that we'll stand then, but we'll
be told about that, I've no doubt. So relax, now, Mrs. Engel.
We've no cause to worry ourselves." She laughed, a shade
too brightly, and touched a cross at her throat with trembling
fingers. "I'll say a prayer to St. Peter; he'll not let us disgrace
him."

Maybe she ought to include St. Christopher, Mrs. Engel
thought. He got you places safely; maybe he got you through
things safely. She didn't know, but she wished again that she
had one of his medals. Then she forgot the medal and everything else, for the car was approaching St. Peter's Square, and
she saw how it teemed with people. "We'll never get there!"
she exclaimed. "There isn't even room to walk!"

But the car ignored the congested Square and swept to
a gateway at its left, where Swiss Guards made splotches of
red and yellow against gray stone. A note from Mrs. Engel's
guidebook leaped to her memory, and she recognized the
entrance they were approaching. It's the Arch of the Bells,
she thought, and we're going through it to see the Pope. She
caught sight of herself in the car mirror, and made a final,
token gesture. Taking her handkerchief, she quickly, almost
with one movement, rubbed off her lipstick.

As Miss Murphy presented her special tickets, the guards at the Arch saluted, and, as the car rolled through it to a courtyard inside, Mrs. Engel bowed to them in return. It's like royalty, she thought. Now they drove up to a wide door, where they waited while a car ahead of them discharged three ladies in long mantillas and a man with a ribbon around his neck, from which hung a gold cross. Other crosses and medals were pinned to the breast of his somber suit. A Papal Count, Mrs. Engel decided, or a Knight of the Realm—no, of Malta, she corrected herself. Well, anyway, he was *someone*, she was sure, and she wondered if he would be in their stand. His car moved on, and it was her own and Miss Murphy's turn to alight. A man with gloves and badge approved their tickets with a low bow, and Mrs. Engel, her heart thumping perceptibly, followed Miss Murphy up a short flight of steps toward the unknown.

Almost at once, there were people. Not guards—not chamberlains, as Mrs. Engel had half expected—but ordinary, everyday people, all in what was unmistakably a tearing hurry. "Where did *they* come from?" Miss Murphy asked, as she and Mrs. Engel headed with the rest down a long stone corridor. Feet sounded behind them, and four nuns with winged coifs like flying birds passed on the double. Six young men in bright red cassocks went by like a flash fire. "Seminarians. They're always rushing," said Miss Murphy. Two

Norwegians and an American soldier skirted Mrs. Engel with the effect of being on skis. "I wonder if we're in the right place," said Miss Murphy, and waved her special tickets for the attention of an official stationed on the way.

"*Si, si,*" he responded. "*Avanti, avanti.*" Mrs. Engel thought he sounded impatient, but she reminded herself that most Italians did.

"*Avanti!*" cried a man with a sword, and this time there was no doubt.

Unconsciously, Miss Murphy increased her speed, infecting Mrs. Engel, and soon they were almost running. Dignity was receding, and more and more people were overtaking them, all with the look of men and women who had just been told that the dam had burst. "Where do they think they're *going?*" asked Miss Murphy, rebounding from the impact of several small but solid little girls in white First Communion dresses.

If Mrs. Engel had an answer, it was smothered by an Italian family that converged on her and bore her through an opening into the arms of a man in a cocked hat. "*Avanti!*" he commanded, and Mrs. Engel found that she was out of the corridor and in the immensity of the church.

"We're all right," said Miss Murphy breathlessly. "We've come around a back way. We're in the transept, and the stand can't be far off."

Although the crowds kept them moving, Mrs. Engel

could recognize, now, where she was. She was near the canopied High Altar, and the dome was just above. She looked up and gasped. From top to bottom, for as far as she could see, the church was hung with blazing red and studded with lighted candelabra, as if scarlet ribbons had been pinned to the arches with diamond brooches, and there, in front of the lamp-lined tomb of St. Peter, she could just see a dais on which stood a tall chair, its pointed back glinting with gold. She stopped dead.

"*Avanti!*" protested a little man, who was behaving as if he were directing a line of fire buckets.

"We go to the *stand*," said Miss Murphy, waving her tickets again.

"*Si, si, va bene,*" said someone soothingly, and Mrs. Engel and Miss Murphy were propelled up a step or two onto a railed platform covered by what seemed to be a low ceiling, and so choked with occupants that Mrs. Engel could only think of what she had heard of the New York subway at the rush hour. But before she could do more than notice that at least the front rows were decorous with long lines of motionless nuns, a hoarse injunction compelled her on. "*Di sopra!*" it said. "*Di sopra.* Up, please, up."

She nudged Miss Murphy, who was standing stock-still. "We have to go up," Mrs. Engel said. Miss Murphy turned, looking as if she were about to cry. "Up," Mrs. Engel repeated. "We go up."

The press of people impelled them to a stairway, narrow and quivering, that ran eerily up behind the platform and led to a tier above it—a balcony, which Mrs. Engel had mistaken for a ceiling. "It's as bad here," said Miss Murphy, like a Celtic Cassandra. "There's no hope for us at all."

Mrs. Engel looked around her. The first rows up here, like those she had noticed below, were neat with the black-and-white of nuns. Over in one corner, the man with all the medals cowered crestfallen, his ladies crushed against him. Anywhere one could sit, people sat, and where they couldn't sit, they stood. "We should have come earlier," said Miss Murphy inadequately.

"*Mi scusi,*" said a Roman matron, squeezing herself into a space where none had existed.

"*Prego,*" said Mrs. Engel, and wished she hadn't.

"Pardon," said an American voice, and a man with three cameras flattened her as he pushed by.

"We should have come earlier," said Miss Murphy again, standing as stiff and weighted as the statue of St. Andrew against which the stand was erected.

"Look!" said Mrs. Engel.

At the very back, on a line with St. Andrew's knees, she had spotted a bench that offered a suggestion of space. She steered Miss Murphy, who seemed incapable of independent action, toward it. It was mainly in possession of the Italian family that had engulfed Mrs. Engel in the corridor. "No, no!" they cried in concerted defense. "We save!"

Mrs. Engel took courage. "*Non capisco*. No understand," she said, and hoped it was all right to fib in church. "Well," she said, when she had inserted herself and Miss Murphy in the space, "this isn't so bad."

The balcony was crammed, but it sloped steeply, and it was possible to see the dais. "And there's no one behind us, so we can stand up to see better," she said. She thought a moment. "I mean if that would be correct. Will people *do* that?"

Miss Murphy looked at the excited crowd about her. "I don't know *what* they'll do," she said through tight lips. "I'd put nothing past them."

Mrs. Engel attempted comfort. "They'll settle down," she said, raising her voice against the chatter of several languages. "They'll be wonderful. Look at all those nice nuns."

Miss Murphy stared stonily at the veils and coifs that had pre-empted the front rows of seats. "Why wouldn't they be nice?" she said. "All in the best places, like that."

"Maybe they got here *very* early," Mrs. Engel offered placatingly.

"I'd not be surprised if they'd slept here," said Miss Murphy witheringly.

Mrs. Engel gave up. Miss Murphy was disappointed, and so was she, but, after all, it was worse for Miss Murphy, because the Pope was *her* Pope. Surely, when the time came, it would be all right. Finally putting aside her ideas of royal boxes and velvet chairs, Mrs. Engel admitted to herself that at least the position of the stand was enviable. It faced the dais below, and when the Pope was there and everyone was quiet, they would see him well. She craned for confirmation and drew a breath at what she saw. The transept was checkered with groups of nuns, priests, children, and—"laymen" she supposed was the word—in orderly, squared-off sections. But away from these, stretching back beyond her vision, were masses and masses of people, so dwarfed by the vast space and distances that they had only the dark, packed quality of a homogeneous sticky substance. "Caviar," Mrs. Engel said to herself. "The church is full of caviar." Above the crowd's blackness, the basilica soared in the brilliance of its decorations like a flaming, protective bird. Under the dome, the chair dominated, still waiting for the hush she was sure would herald the coming of the Pope. Dotted near it were Swiss Guards, their uniforms—so improbable by daylight—now as right as votive candles.

"Michelangelo knew what he was doing when he designed

those uniforms," Mrs. Engel murmured, to distract Miss Murphy, who sniffed.

"I've read that he did it one day when he was annoyed," she said coldly. "And whoever designed this stand must have been in the same state. It's not safe. Listen to that, will you?"

The stairs were creaking under the strain of heavily ascending feet. "Someone ought to stop them," said Mrs. Engel. "It was full long ago."

A young Irish priest standing near heard her and grinned. "In Italy, there's no such word as full," he said.

"If you ask *me*," said Miss Murphy, "the nuns are the worst. There's twice as many now as there were."

The priest chuckled. "They have a system," he said. "They spread themselves out, with their veils and all, and then move close together when other nuns come. They're a caution!"

They talk about them as if they were *people*, Mrs. Engel noted, amazed, but she supposed it was like being in a family. However, she argued to herself, they surely had more right to good places than—well, someone like herself. Or *sight-seers*, she added scathingly as two stolid British tourists, complete with binoculars, increased the standees. If the nuns had their rights, then so had Miss Murphy hers, and she ought to assert them. Mrs. Engel was getting confused, but she was also getting angry. She glared at the binoculars and turned to Miss Murphy, who had subsided into misery.

Mrs. Engel couldn't bear it. "Get down there, Miss Murphy," she ordered peremptorily. "Get right down there in front."

"Me?" said Miss Murphy, startled. "There's no room there."

"*Make* it!" said Mrs. Engel. "Everyone else does, and you have more right. Go *on*. Tell them your sister's a nun." Miss Murphy looked uncertain. "*Per favore, attenzione,*" said Mrs. Engel to the air. "*La sorella della signorina——*" She stopped. "I don't know the Italian for 'nun,' " she said, "but you go *on down.*"

Miss Murphy, suddenly spurred, thrust herself forward. Mrs. Engel watched as she edged and pressed and insinuated herself, inch by inch, down through people, between people, until she was miraculously in a corner of the lower tier, by the railing, where at first she clung, and then knelt, to lean over it for an unobstructed view. Mrs. Engel sighed with relief.

"Why don't you have a go at it yourself?" asked the young priest, who had been watching with amusement.

Mrs. Engel shook her head. "I couldn't," she said, and hoped he would understand. "You see, I'm not a Catholic."

The priest smiled. "Better stay where you are now, anyway," he said. "It's almost time Holy Father was here."

Mrs. Engel froze. In her concern for Miss Murphy, she had almost forgotten the Pope, and he was coming. She straightened her hat and tried to wedge herself more firmly onto the bench. Soon everything would be quiet, she knew, and she wouldn't want to move then or disturb anyone.

"*Mama!*" cried the Italian family beside her, and reached ecstatic hands toward a panting old woman, hung with rosaries, who made her way to them. They pulled her down to the bench, almost obliterating Mrs. Engel, and burst into the volubility of people reunited after many years. "They'll stop any moment now," Mrs. Engel told herself, as she was pushed to the very end of the bench. She thought of the hush, and the Pope borne high to the dais, and she gripped her hands together to stop them from shaking. Then, all at once, as if some wordless signal had been given, the shuffling and the chatter were arrested, and a strange intensity took their place, as if something unseen were gathering itself in. From far back in the church came a murmur.

"He's coming," said the young priest, almost to himself, and Mrs. Engel saw his face whiten. The murmur rose and became a clamor: "*Viva!*" Mrs. Engel heard. "*Viva il Papa!*" The cry rose and was repeated. "*Viva il Papa!*" screamed a woman near her in the stand, and Mrs. Engel felt the crowd go mad around her. Everyone was standing, leaning forward; the shouting grew until it was a wall of sound. The Pope was there, below her, she thought, and she couldn't *see* him. Some people clambered onto the benches, to stand. She tried to climb onto hers, but there was no room there. She was in a well, she thought, a tight, dark well, while the people around her, who made the well, roared an acclamation to the Pope she couldn't see. Then the noise lessened, and a voice floated out and up. The Pope was speaking, she realized, and she strained frantically to hear him. A half-understood phrase here and there told her he was welcoming the groups below in their several languages, going from one to another quite easily. Then, almost before she could take them in, the words came in English, pure and almost unaccented: ". . . our blessing to you and all your family and friends. . . ."

"Oh, *please*," she heard herself say aloud. "I want to *see*." She actually whimpered, and, from behind her, hands clasped her waist, and she was lifted into the air. She had one dazed glimpse of the figure in white rising from the chair on the dais before she was put down again. She turned and saw who had lifted her. It was the father of the Italian family, who was standing above her on the bench. "*Mille grazie*," she said, but he didn't hear her. He was looking out and down, his middle-aged eyes childlike with tears. The people were now getting down from the benches. Mrs. Engel felt panic. It's over, she thought. It's all over, and I've missed the blessing. But no one left, and the complete hush that Mrs. Engel had imagined would come when the Pope first entered came at last. All around her, and down in the church, the thousands dropped to their knees as one person, with a curious sound, like snow slipping from a roof. For a moment, Mrs. Engel stood alone, looking over the bowed heads before her, and now she saw the figure in white clearly. She saw the sweeping sign of the cross, and, light though the hand was that made it, it seemed to fill the length and breadth of the church. Then she, too, knelt.

The next half-hour was a blur. Mrs. Engel knew vaguely when the Pope left the dais and was carried down the nave; she followed his progress by the diminishment of the cheering. It stopped, and he was gone. Finally, Miss Murphy appeared, pale and tear-stained, her mantilla awry, her parcel of medals clutched in a death grip. Together they made their way out to the courtyard, where the car was waiting, and rode back to the hotel in shaken silence.

Mr. Engel was in the lobby, ready to take them to lunch. Miss Murphy refused. "I'm destroyed," she said. "I'll just have a cup of tea in my room above." She looked at them both. "It wasn't the way I thought it would be, it wasn't the way at all," she said. "All that pushing and shoving and screaming at him, and himself a saint!"

Mrs. Engel thought back on the shouting and the intensity and the tears. She touched Miss Murphy's hand. "Maybe that's the reason for it," she said.

Miss Murphy's eyes filled. "Well, anyway, we saw him," she said, and an unexpected humor creased her face into a smile, "in spite of our special seats."

The Engels went alone to the garden for lunch. "What did *you* do this morning?" Mrs. Engel asked after she had given an account of hers.

"I saw the Pope," said Mr. Engel.

Mrs. Engel flushed. "I don't think it's very funny to joke about it, after all I've told you."

"I'm not joking," said Mr. Engel, prodding a piece of pastry. "I went to St. Peter's and saw the Pope. Here." He took a medal from his pocket and slid it across the table to her.

She took it up. "It's a St. Christopher," she said.

"Isn't that what you wanted?"

"Of course."

"It's blessed," said Mr. Engel severely, "so don't lose it."

"But how? How did you *get* it blessed?"

"I told you. You wanted a medal, so I got one and took it to St. Peter's."

"But how did you get in? It was jammed."

"There was a crowd," said Mr. Engel judiciously, "but I went in, in back of it."

"*How* in back of it?"

"The crowd was all in the big center aisle," said Mr. Engel

patiently, "but the side ones were fairly empty. I just walked up one till I got to where the Pope was speaking. When he was all through, he walked around by the railing where I was, and that's when I saw him near to."

"You mean you were *close* to him?"

"Not very—about like that." He indicated a tub of geraniums some six feet away.

"You mean without a ticket, without waiting, without *anything*, you just walked in and saw him?"

"Certainly."

Mrs. Engel drank a glass of water. "What was he like, close to? Were you impressed?"

Mr. Engel retreated from the query. "I don't know what you mean by 'impressed.'"

Mrs. Engel changed her approach. "I just meant *imagine* seeing him so *close*. What a shame you didn't have a camera."

Mr. Engel took on what his wife called his Rock of New England look. "I wouldn't have used it," he said stiffly.

"But why not?"

"It wouldn't have been respectful," said Mr. Engel.

His wife looked down at her plate, satisfied with his answer. It was how she had felt about wearing lipstick, only she couldn't explain why. She turned the St. Christopher medal in her hand; if it had been blessed, she suddenly thought, then so had Mr. Engel. She looked at him and smiled, and then put the medal into her handbag.

Mr. Engel caught the movement. "Be careful of it, now," he said. "Don't lose it."

"I won't," said Mrs. Engel. "I promise I won't."

$\mathcal{U}$ntil just before they left Rome, Mrs. Engel had thought of her husband's new secretary as a voice on the telephone— a serene, pleasant, obliging voice, calm in crisis (such as the time Mrs. Engel had telephoned to say that the Frigidaire was on fire) and precise in the delivery of messages. Apart from that, Mrs. Engel knew only that she was married, that her husband was something in the Navy, only not a sailor, and that Mr. Engel found her extremely quick and capable. Mrs. Engel, too, had found her helpful, particularly in arranging some of the many small details that had been part of the preparation for this trip abroad. "We really must bring her something from Rome," she had said to her husband before they sailed from New York, and then forgotten her until now. They were in a sort of gift shop on the Via Sistina, waiting while the shopkeeper assembled their purchases and set about wrapping them all together in the paper that she hated to part with but that she had found Americans expected.

It was noon; the shopping had taken a long time and the mounting heat penetrated the shop, increasing their weariness and making Mrs. Engel long for lunch and the siesta that even Mr. Engel had come to accept as a necessary part of their routine. "Well, anyway," she said, trying to ease one foot a little out of its shoe, "I honestly think that's everyone." She ran a pencil down her list. "Yes, that's the lot." She folded the list and put it in her bag.

"Mrs. Leech," said her husband.

"Mrs. *Who?*"

"Mrs. Leech. My secretary. It was you who said we should. You told me to remind you."

"Oh, Mrs. *Leech!* Heavens, yes, of course we must! She was so helpful—all that telephoning, and the Salvation Army."

"The what?" asked her husband.

"Just some bundles. She had them picked up." As Mr. Engel looked at her, she added quickly, "It was only a phone call. Well, now, what shall we get her? *"Una momento,"* she said to the shopkeeper, who was trying to stretch a rubber band around one of the parcels. *"Una momento, per favore, signora.* We want—*Non finito, scusi."*

The shopkeeper, who from the first had countered Mrs. Engel's Italian with firm English, continued wearily to do so. "Take your time, madame," she said, with only a slight glance at the clock.

"She wants to close for lunch," Mrs. Engel said to her husband, "but it won't take long. Let me see. . . ." She began to move about the shop, although she now knew its contents practically by heart. "What about a handbag?"

"I think she has handbags," Mr. Engel said.

"Well, *of course* she has handbags, but she hasn't got one from Rome, has she? What about this?" She held up a large red wicker object vaguely resembling a picnic hamper. It was decorated with cucumbers and bananas in bright green and yellow felt.

"No," said Mr. Engel.

"No? But all the young girls love these. They're so gay with

cotton dresses and things. Of course, if she *isn't* a young girl—
I only know her voice, and that doesn't sound especially
young, now I think of it. Maybe there's something more con-
servative." Her eye fell on a leather pouched affair, stenciled
with sunflowers. "This is useful," she said. "She could carry
things in it—knitting, or books. It's just right for an older
woman."

"She's about twenty-three," said Mr. Engel.

"Then the red one would be perfect."

"It's too big," he said. "They're both too big."

Mrs. Engel put a hand to her forehead, and pushed her
hat a little out of place. "But all the bags are big now. It's the
fashion. Mine is a big bag."

Mr. Engel said nothing. His wife sighed. *"Scusi, signora?"*
She held out the red bag. *"Una simile, ma una poco piccolo?"*

The shopkeeper half closed her eyes. "We have only what
you see," she replied. "We have nothing small."

Mrs. Engel shot a triumphant look at her husband. "No
one has!" she said to him. "All the bags in all the shops are
big. Well, if we don't get her this, what *will* we get her?"

"I don't know," Mr. Engel said. "Anything. Only not a
big thing."

"Anything, only not a big thing." Mrs. Engel put the bag
aside and looked musingly around the shop. "Why not a big
thing?" she asked suddenly.

"She's small," Mr. Engel said.

"Well, for pity's sake, what has *that* got to do with it? Just because a person is small . . ." She stopped and looked at him. "I'm small. I like big things. Is she *my* size?"

"About," her husband said.

"Well, then." She picked up the red bag again, hooked one arm through the handle, and faced him for approval. After a minute, she put the bag back on the counter. "All right, dear," she said. "Let's think of something else."

She saw a tray of necklaces and began to turn them over. "Well, why didn't I see this before!" She held up a long string of beads—dark-blue flecked with gold, and knotted with green silk. "It's beautiful," she said. "I think it's just beautiful. *Molto bello.*" She smiled at the shopkeeper. "*Molto bello per una ragazza? Quanta costa?*"

"Ten thousand lire," the shopkeeper said.

"How much is that?" Mrs. Engel whispered to her husband.

"Sixteen dollars," the shopkeeper said.

"Well," said Mrs. Engel. "It's worth it just to get done, and it *is* beautiful." She started to hand it to the shopkeeper. "You like it, don't you?" she asked Mr. Engel.

He shifted against the counter where he was leaning. "I think it's a bit heavy," he said.

Mrs. Engel stared at him. "Heavy. *Heavy?* They're ce-

ramic, they're light as light, they're like *nothing*. Feel them!"
She held them out.

He shook his head. "I don't mean the weight. They just
look too heavy—too long, too . . . I don't think she wears
things like that."

Mrs. Engel regarded him closely. "What kind of things
does she wear?"

"I don't know. She always looks very nice—very neat, I
mean. I don't think she wears jewelry at all. She wears a wedding ring." He paused. Mrs. Engel waited. "And a wrist-
watch," he added. "Sometimes she wears a little locket."

"A locket," said Mrs. Engel. She let the ceramic beads
filter through her fingers and back onto the tray.

"This will be all, then?" the shopkeeper said, and nodded
toward the large parcel on the counter.

"*Si*," said Mrs. Engel. "*Finito*."

The shopkeeper handed the rather insecure and unwieldy
package to her, and gave Mr. Engel the bill. Mrs. Engel waited
while he paid it, studied the slip for the customs, and then put
it in his wallet and the wallet in his pocket. He took the parcel
from her. "Thanks," he said to the shopkeeper as they started
to leave.

"*Prego, signore*," said the shopkeeper. "*Tante grazie*."

As they walked up the street to their hotel, Mrs. Engel
noticed that the other shops were closed. "We kept her awfully

late," she said. "But I did want to get done, and now we still have Mrs. Leech." An unshuttered window caught her attention. "Look," she said. "What about that?" She pointed to a belt hanging on display. It was shiny and black, and silver sea horses rode gaily around it. "That really is sweet. And *different*. I'm glad now we didn't get the bag or the beads, really I am." She sighed with relief. "I'll just come and get it when they're open again."

She looked at Mr. Engel and then stood still on the narrow sidewalk. "*Now* what is it?" she asked.

"Nothing," he said. "Come on, people can't get around you."

"Is the *belt* too big? Is *that* what it is?"

"Yes. No, no, it's fine—well, yes, then, I think it is. It would go round her twice."

"*Twice?*"

Her husband took her arm and started her walking again. "You can take a belt *in*," she said.

"She has a very small waist," Mr. Engel said. "You can put your hands around it."

The Engels had lunch in the umbrella-shaded garden of their hotel. Afterward they went up to their room, which was prepared, as always at that hour, for the afternoon rest—curtains, drawn against the sun, gently darkening the room, the day covers folded back on the beds. Mrs. Engel took the package from her husband and put it away, and then began slowly to undress. Mr. Engel retired to the bathroom and after some time emerged, rid of everything but his shorts, and settled into his bed.

Mrs. Engel spoke to him for the first time since they had come upstairs. "How do you know?" she asked.

"How do I know what?"

"Mrs. Leech's waist. How do you know you can put your hands around it?"

"My hands? I didn't say *my* hands!"

"You said, 'She has a very small waist. You can put your hands around it.'"

Mr. Engel twisted in the bed. "For Pete's sake," he said, "I didn't mean it that way. I meant it the way anyone does. I meant a *person* could."

"But how do you know *that*?"

Mr. Engel put an arm over his face to shut out a pencil of sunlight that had pierced a space between the curtains. "It was one day in the outer office," he said. "The girls were having a break. They make themselves tea out there. They have tea now, instead of coffee."

"I know that. You told me."

"Well, and I was passing through and they were all laughing, and I stopped, and they were kidding her about being so small."

"How small is she?" Mrs. Engel asked, with no particular emphasis. "You make her sound like a midget."

"She isn't," he said. "She isn't short at all. It's just that she's *made* small. Small hands. Small feet." He stopped.

"Go on," said his wife.

"So they were kidding her, and they bet she could put her hands around her waist and have them meet, so she tried."

"And did they?"

"Pretty near. So I just thought if hers could—"

"Yours could," Mrs. Engel finished for him.

"A *person's* could," he said. "I wasn't even near her. I was just over in a corner watching."

"I see."

"So you see what I mean about her being small? It isn't height or weight. She probably weighs as much as you do."

"I weigh exactly one hundred and fourteen pounds," Mrs. Engel said.

"Well, that's what I mean," he said and yawned. "Are you going to take your nap?"

"In a minute or two. You go ahead." She drew the curtains close, and the one beam of sun disappeared. Mr. Engel turned over and pulled the sheet over his face. Mrs. Engel finished undressing, and put on a cool robe. There was just enough light in the room for her to see herself dimly in the long mirror set in the wardrobe door, and she stood in front of it and examined her reflected self. Not fat, not thin. Not short, not tall. Not old, not young. She put her hands on each side of her waist and pressed, but the settled thickness resisted them. That was it, she thought; it wasn't weight, or being made small—she remembered her husband's words—it was being young.

She went over in her mind the scene in the big outer office —the girls clustered like flowers, laughing over their teamaking, and Mr. Engel, heavy, middle-aged, coming on them unexpectedly, stopping to watch them. Especially watching the smallest one, the one that was always neat and nicely dressed, with her wedding ring bright on her small hand, and a locket prim against her small throat. . . . All at once, Mrs. Engel knew how he had watched. It was the way she looked at a dress in a shop window, a ruffled and fragile dress, made for moonlight and dancing. She couldn't wear such dresses now and she had sense enough to know it, but that didn't stop her from loving to look at them. Even when they belonged to someone else, she thought, she couldn't help watching them, any more than she could help wishing—wishing and remembering.

Mrs. Engel pulled her robe about her and sat on her bed looking over at her husband, who was now sound asleep. She put her hand gently on his shrouded shoulder. "We'll find her something," she whispered. "Something neat and nice and very, very small."

Then she lay down and very soon she, too, was asleep.

MR. ENGEL'S EYE

*T*he terrace of the restaurant in the Pincio, in Rome, was appropriately rustic, but the inner rooms through which the Engels passed on their way out after lunch were definitely urban. Pink-and-white striped wallpaper served as a foil for gilt and oak and dangling glass, and Mrs. Engel decided that, if there was such a style as Baroque Mission, this was it. She stopped in the hall and pointed to a golden cupid bearing a tray of marble fruit. "There!" she said to Mr. Engel. "That's what I mean about Grace Wetherall!"

Ordinarily, Mr. Engel was able to follow his wife's thought associations without more than a moment's adjustment, but a morning in the Borghese Gardens and an off-diet luncheon had slowed his responses. He looked at the bulbous *amorino* and found no connection. "My present for her," Mrs. Engel explained. *"That's* the sort of thing I want to bring her."

"I thought you had a present for her. I thought we had all the presents for everybody."

"Not for Grace. Well, yes, I did get that billfold with the Paisley lining for her, but it's not right."

"Why isn't it?" asked Mr. Engel, moving Mrs. Engel out of range of a waiter who was passing with a tray of cream-topped pastries. "I thought it was fine."

"It isn't amusing," said Mrs. Engel. "Grace likes things to be amusing. She took a course or something once."

"You mean she likes things like this?" Mr. Engel asked wonderingly.

"It isn't exactly that she *likes* them," his wife answered. "If she liked them it would be bad taste, but if they amuse her it's all right."

"How do you know when she's amused?" asked Mr. Engel.

"She tells you. I mean, she doesn't say, 'Have you seen my shell pincushion?' She says, 'Have you seen my *absurd* shell pincushion?' Then you know."

"Oh," said Mr. Engel. "Well, let's get back to the hotel. Want to taxi or walk?"

"Walk," said Mrs. Engel. "We need to."

Outside the restaurant, the Pincio was studded with busts of ancient dignitaries wearing expressions that varied from smoldering indignation to pure rage. "Are *they* amusing?" Mr. Engel asked his wife, who then stopped and pondered.

"I'm not sure," she said finally. "I think they ought to have plush on them, or be painted pink, or something. But it is hard to know. You have to have an eye for amusing things, the way *you* have an eye for good ones."

"Me?" said Mr. Engel. "When did I have an eye for good things?"

"Lots of times," said Mrs. Engel as they walked on. "Like in Florence when you picked out the Donatello plaque."

"Well—I liked it," said Mr. Engel defensively.

"That's what I'm saying," said his wife. "You didn't know it was good. You just picked it out instinctively. And you picked out the cherub heads in the Chapel, and *they* were good."

Mr. Engel looked uncomfortable. "I just thought they were cute," he said. "I wasn't being artistic about them."

His wife looked up at him. "I don't know why you act as though I were accusing you of something," she said. "I think it's wonderful that you have an eye."

The Engels reached the road that would lead them past the Villa Medici and on to their hotel. Mrs. Engel stopped, and looked back. The clouds were banked in sculptured masses, and the trees made dark patterns against the delphinium blue of the sky. Up on the hill the Engels had left, the cypresses stood like cowled monks, tall and sparse and remote. "Michelangelo does the clouds, and Donatello carves the cypresses," Mrs. Engel said to herself, taking Mr. Engel's arm.

The shaded avenue was quiet; not many Italians walked there at that hour of the siesta, but a few leaned lazily over the wall that ran along it, gazing down at their city, below. They live here, Mrs. Engel thought, watching them, but the young people look at it as if they had never seen it before, and the old as if they might never see it again. Her arm tightened in Mr. Engel's. "After our nap," she said, "I'm going to look for a thing for Grace, and then I'm not going to do anything till we leave but just *be* here."

"Good," said Mr. Engel, as they continued their leisurely way.

"Only, I wish I could find some amusing place to look in," Mrs. Engel said. "Like that market in Paris, or the Caledonian one in London. Grace likes things you pick up in odd places."

Mr. Engel was growing sleepy. "Give her the billfold," he said through a yawn, "and tell her you picked it up in St. Peter's."

Mrs. Engel did not smile. "I wish there was a Roman market," she said. "But maybe I can find a thrift shop, or something. I could *say* it was a market—only, I'd say it in Italian. I'd say '*uno mercato di Roma,*' and if Grace didn't understand, I'd translate." She quickened her pace, as though the thought had spurred her, and if Mr. Engel sighed a little as he followed suit, she did not hear him.

The next Sunday morning, the hotel porter helped the Engels into the hotel limousine and gave the driver voluble directions.

"What did he tell him?" asked Mr. Engel, as the car started off.

"Just which bridge to cross to the market, I think," said Mrs. Engel. "And to wait there for us. He said it might be hard to find a taxi back on Sunday morning."

"I don't see why we have to go on a Sunday anyway," said

Mr. Engel, clinging to the strap as the car circled the Trinita and headed toward the river.

"Because they only have it on Sunday," said his wife. "That's its name, *Mercato di Domenica*—the Sunday Market. I told you. Every Sunday morning, all these Italians come from everywhere and bring all these things they don't want, and all these other Italians come and buy them. No matter how awful they are, the porter said, someone can use them."

"That sounds like secondhand stuff," said Mr. Engel with some distaste. "You don't want that, do you?"

"No," said Mrs. Engel, "but they have antiques, too. He said all the decorators go there and buy things and fix them up and sell them again for thousands. He said he was sure I'd find a thing for Grace. He said they have *everything*. Wasn't it wonderful that I thought of asking him where to go?" She beamed at Mr. Engel, and then became serious. "Now," she said, as the car approached the Tiber, "what we have to remember is not to pay the first price they ask. They don't like it if you do."

"That's silly," said Mr. Engel. "Who told you that?"

"The porter. He said they like to bargain. It spoils it for them if you don't. He said to let them say a price, and then offer half that; then they'll say a middle price, and that's it."

Mr. Engel frowned. "Do you know enough Italian for all that?" he asked.

"I think so," his wife replied. "I know numbers if they're not too high, and I can say things like *'Non posso'* and *'Va bene'* to fill in. I couldn't haggle, but I can bargain the way the porter said to."

She steadied herself as the car swerved to cross a bridge that led to a wide, open street, where the Sunday Market was spread—a fantastic picnic, swarmed over by happy, vociferous ants and flooded by the sun, already high in a cloudless sky.

"Stay *with* me," said Mr. Engel, as they left the car and Mrs. Engel made a sort of plunge forward. "If I lost you here, I'd never find you."

"I'd find *you*," said Mrs. Engel, but she slowed obediently as they reached the rows of stalls. Confetti mounds of clothing lay on the ground, glassware made splintered rainbows in the blinding light, and blinking mirrors on unsteady tables sent wavering, beckoning signals to the crowd. Feathers waved enticingly from hats heaped beside pots and pans as bright as they were dented. Furniture loomed behind stacks of china and suitcases, and the coils and springs of a tangle of worn electrical equipment quivered with serpentine allure. It was all gay and oddly brave, and in the midst of it—but a little to one side, as if in apology—lay six hopeless pairs of shoes and three rusted locks, their only merit the abject neatness of their arrangement. "No matter how bad, somebody needs, so somebody buys," the hotel porter had said, and Mrs. Engel's throat tightened as the words came back to her.

Men and women were pushing eagerly around her, and though for the most part they were in drab working clothes or greenish black, they all looked to her as though they were carrying balloons.

"They're excited when they can buy *anything*," she said to Mr. Engel. "It isn't just a market to them—it's a *festa*. Look at the stallkeepers!"

The stallkeepers wore fancy hats. Some were cocked hats made of newspapers, fashioned against the scalding sun. One or two were probably worn by habit, like the ancient stove-pipe on the head of an old man who sat on a high, laddered chair above his stall, as impervious to stares as a figure on the Sistine ceiling. Other hats were swashbuckling jokes—slapped-on wilted velvet-and-brocade toques obviously snatched from the piles for sale. A heavily mustached man grinned under a red satin tricorn, and, for all his grinning, looked like a Veronese magistrate, while a pointed green pyramid of a hat turned his sweating young helper into a Renaissance apprentice.

"It's in their blood," said Mrs. Engel.

"What is?" asked her husband.

"Velvet," said Mrs. Engel. "And silk, and hats with ornaments. They don't look silly in them, even when they try to.

It's what they used to wear, and what they'd like to wear now, and that's why they look all right in them."

"Well, fine," said Mr. Engel. "But what about Grace Wetherall? Have you seen anything for her yet?"

"I haven't looked yet," said Mrs. Engel. "This is just the secondhand section. We have to find the antiques."

The antique section, when the Engels found it, was very much like the secondhand one. The chief difference was that, while the secondhand wares were offered with some pretense of their being intact, the antiques were displayed with regal emphasis on their disrepair. Also, the *festa* spirit was diminished, and there were more Americans in evidence. People came here for a purpose, rather than a need, Mrs. Engel thought, but the stalls stacked with crumbling, unrelated objects rekindled her enthusiasm.

"Look," she said, and pulled Mr. Engel close to a stand where two young men wearing pastel pullovers with contrasting scarves were conferring about the severed halves of a tall polychrome candlestick. "Decorators," she said, in a whisper. "Just as the porter said. They'll make lamps out of it, or end tables."

"Well, don't stare at them," said Mr. Engel.

"I'm *not*," said Mrs. Engel. "I just wanted to show you."

"Well, come on," said Mr. Engel, but Mrs. Engel lagged,

her attention caught by some small figures, too realistic to be dolls, tossed on a rat's nest of bedraggled lace.

"Do you suppose they were puppets, like the ones in Sicily?" she asked Mr. Engel, who shook his head.

One of the young men with the candlestick caught the words. "My *dear*," he said to Mrs. Engel, making her start, "have you *seen* the Sicilian puppets? They're absolute *heaven*, aren't they?" He touched one of the figures on the pile of lace. "But these aren't puppets. They're from a crèche—part of a group around a crib, you know. Of course, they're fun, too. I mean in their own way." He smiled brightly, and returned to his candlestick.

Mrs. Engel picked up one of the figures—a woman in peasant dress. The linen blouse was brown with age, but intricately sewn and pleated, and the laced bodice still showed a faint crimson. A hand and a foot were missing, but the head, which turned to look over one shoulder, was perfect. But there was nothing of fun in the carved and tinted face. Instead, it held an expression of half-incredulous awe. Of course! Mrs. Engel thought. She was looking at the manger.

"*Quanta costa?*" Mrs. Engel asked the stallkeeper, who was appraising her. "I mean, *che domanda?* That means 'What are you asking?'" she said, in an undertone, to Mr. Engel. "The porter told me to say it."

"*Dodici cento,*" said the stallkeeper.

"Twelve hundred lire," Mrs. Engel translated for her husband, and steeled herself to bargain. "Eleven—I mean *undici cento*," she said firmly.

"*H'oh*kay," said the stallkeeper, and took the money that Mr. Engel produced.

"He didn't ask a middle price," said Mrs. Engel when they had moved on.

"You didn't give him much chance," said Mr. Engel. "If that's for Grace, why don't we go now? It's getting pretty hot."

It *was* hot, Mrs. Engel agreed, and her excitement had flagged, but she looked at the figure she had just bought, at the fragment of ribbon binding the carved hair behind ears that were flat and exquisite, and she hesitated. "I'll just look at one more——" she said, and broke off. "There!" she exclaimed. "*There* it is!"

"There's what?" asked Mr. Engel, startled.

"Grace's present," said Mrs. Engel, her voice higher. "I knew I'd find it!"

"People are *looking* at you," said Mr. Engel. "What do you see?"

Mrs. Engel pointed, speechless. High up on a stand, balanced on a topple of books and ironwork and maps and fans, was a brightly colored picture of a boy with a page's haircut and jerkin, holding in his arms an unidentifiable animal that

might have been a dog or a boar or a medieval invention. It
had a rodent nose and sharp ears, and it peered insanely over
a clockface inexplicably set somewhere in the neighborhood
of the boy's stomach. The animal was a rich brown, the boy's
jerkin was red, yellow, and blue, and the background was
green. Encasing this nightmare splendor was a wide gilt
frame.

"That's *it*," said Mrs. Engel, recovering. She waved to the
stallkeeper. "*Per favore, signore*—the picture. The *ragazzo*
with the dog—*con il cane*," she said wildly.

The stallkeeper shrugged, but followed her pointing finger,
and, grunting, lifted the object down, and put it in her hands,
which sagged under its surprising weight. "It isn't a picture,"
she said in amazement. "It's a real clock!"

The object was about a foot square. The clock's works ex-
tended five or six inches at the back, and were enclosed, along
with the clockface, in a wooden case with a glass front. It
looked, Mrs. Engel thought, as if it had been a picture first,
and someone had decided to turn it into a clock. She examined
it more closely. "Look at the boy's eyes," she said to Mr. Engel.
"They're glass! Someone cut out the painted ones and stuck
in doll's eyes!"

Mr. Engel took the clock from her. "You'll drop it," he
said, and set it on a chest with three drawers missing.

It's perfect for Grace, Mrs. Engel thought, recovering

the crèche doll, which she had put down. It'll be wonderful to tell her that I just picked it up in the Sunday Market.

Mrs. Engel turned to look at the clock again, and found it surrounded by a group of fascinated Italians, who were leaning over Mr. Engel's shoulder in wordless contemplation. A plump woman with soft, envious eyes gestured her admiration. *"Molto bello, mo-oolto bello per la casa,"* she said, giving the vowels the note of a mourning dove.

"Of course, the clock is worthless," said a smallish man, in crisp English. "But the frame is fifteenth-century. Grab it for the frame."

One of the young men who had been looking at the candlestick appeared at Mrs. Engel's side. "Well, if you don't buy it, *I* will," he said. "It's *too* amusing."

Mrs. Engel signaled decisively to the stallkeeper. *"Che domanda?"* she said. The crowd straightened to a hushed attention.

"It's the frame you want," the smallish man reminded her. "It's a collector's piece. Get the frame and throw the clock away."

Mrs. Engel tried to ignore him. *"Che domanda?"* she repeated.

"Dodici mille lire," the stallkeeper said, and folded his arms.

The crowd looked at Mrs. Engel and moved in a little.

This time, she knew, she must leave room for a middle bid. She hesitated, making mental subtractions. "He wants twelve *thousand*," she whispered to Mr. Engel, to gain time.

"Offer him less," said the smallish man, still at her elbow.

"I *know*," said Mrs. Engel. "I'm *thinking!*"

A few minutes later, Mrs. Engel was hurrying along beside her husband, who was carrying the clock and walking rather faster than usual.

"You gave him twelve thousand lire before I could bargain," she said. "You just handed it to him. You didn't even offer him ten thousand first!"

"I don't know the Italian for 'ten,'" said Mr. Engel. "You told me he wanted twelve thousand, so I gave him twelve thousand."

"But he was *disappointed*," said Mrs. Engel. "And so was everyone else. They *murmured*, like the crowds in Shakespeare."

Mr. Engel did not reply, but continued his rapid walk, looking to neither right nor left—like a dog that has an important bone to bury, Mrs. Engel thought, and is afraid another dog will snatch it. Was Mr. Engel afraid someone would snatch the clock? "No one's going to take it from you," she said, "so you needn't clutch it like that. It's just an amusing thing. It hasn't any value, as——"

She broke off, and almost tripped. She had forgotten Mr. Engel's eye. Mr. Engel had an instinct; when he picked something out, it was good. She hastened to catch up with him, and then she remembered the small man who had stood beside her. "The frame is fifteenth century. Grab it for the frame," he had said. Mr. Engel must have done just that—instinctively, since he had been paying no attention to the man. Well, she would give the clock to Grace, and find an antique mirror, or something, for the frame. "It's a fifteenth-century piece that we found in Rome," she heard herself saying (or that *Mr.* Engel had found, she should probably say), but before she could crystallize this, they were at the car and Mr. Engel was resisting the driver's attempt to help him with the clock. "I'll hold it," he said as he got in, and when the car started he put it on his knees and pored over it.

Mrs. Engel watched him with shining eyes. "It's true then, about the frame," she said.

"Frame?" said Mr. Engel vaguely.

"What that man said—that it was a collector's piece."

"I didn't hear him," said Mr. Engel, opening the glass front delicately and nodding toward the driver. "Tell him to go slow, will you?"

Mrs. Engel complied, and returned to the subject. "Then you picked it out yourself," she said. "I knew you did!"

"Picked out what?" asked Mr. Engel, absorbedly moving one of the clock's hands.

"The frame, the fifteenth-century frame," said his wife, touching it for emphasis.

Mr. Engel looked at the frame without interest. "I didn't notice it," he said.

Mrs. Engel let a moment pass in silence. "But you noticed something," she said then. "You must have."

"Well, yes," said Mr. Engel. He turned the clock over and carefully exposed its works. "Look," he said. "This was once a pendulum clock. There were wires *here,* and when the clock was running, they connected *here* and made the eyes move."

"The eyes?" said Mrs. Engel.

"The eyes in the boy's head. They moved back and forth when the clock ticked." He turned it face up again, and manipulated something at its back, and Mrs. Engel saw the boy's eyes turn horribly from left to right and right to left. "If I can find a clockmaker who understands these things," said Mr. Engel softly, "I think he could make it work again. Or if I could find the right parts, I could do it myself."

So that was what it was, Mrs. Engel realized. Not Mr. Engel's eye but his passion for things that did things, like his watch that told him the year and the month, though he already knew them.

"But the frame," she said, not giving up. "Couldn't it be valuable, if it's what the man said?"

"I wouldn't know," said Mr. Engel, "but I doubt it. Those stallmen aren't fools. They know pretty well what they've got."

"But if it *is* valuable," said his wife doggedly, "could it come off the clock to make a mirror, maybe?"

Mr. Engel ran a tentative finger over the frame. "I wouldn't risk it," he said. "Something might break." He closed the glass front, and lapsed into a rapturous brooding.

He loves it, Mrs. Engel thought. He loves it, and he has forgotten all about Grace Wetherall, and it would have been so perfect for her. Of course, she reflected, lifting the crèche figure from her lap, where it was lying, I could still give her this. But as she smoothed the threadbare apron and touched the tiny listening ears, she remembered Grace's high laugh and knew she wouldn't give it to her, or to anyone. She was going to keep it herself, and put it under the tree at Christmas, where it belonged, and she would just have to remind Mr. Engel about Grace Wetherall. She turned with the words at her lips, but something in his attitude held them back. She watched his hands as they treasured the clock, and then she let herself relax against the cushions. I'll give Grace the billfold, she decided, and tell her I thought it was amusing to bring her something practical.

The chauffeur took a corner too fast, and the clock tilted on Mr. Engel's knees. Mrs. Engel leaned forward and spoke to the driver. "*Attento!*" she said sharply. "*Molto piu lento.*" She put a protective hand on Mr. Engel's. "It's all right," she said. "I told him again to go slow."

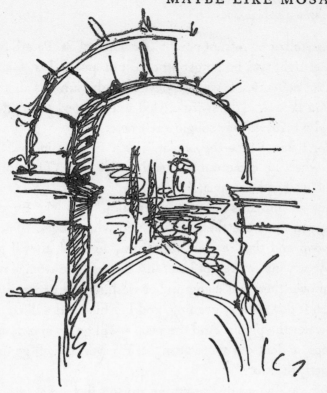

*T*he visit of Mr. and Mrs. Engel to Rome was drawing to a close. Mrs. Engel stood on the balcony of their hotel room and looked out over the city. The Via Sistina below was now as familiar to her as a street at home, and the Spanish Steps

had become her own front porch. The dome of St. Peter's far
off to her right was no longer an object of awe to her, but a
shelter for memories. It was early evening, the sun was almost
gone, and all around the swifts circled and swooped, their cries
thin and wistful as they sought their nests.

"I don't know how they do it," Mrs. Engel said to Mr.
Engel, when he came out to stand beside her. "They just
fly at the wall and disappear."

"They go into slits between the stones," said Mr. Engel.

"But you can't see them do it," said Mrs. Engel. "They
just swoop and they're gone. It's funny to think they'll go
on doing it when we're not here, just the way the woman on
the roof over there will hang up her washing every morning,
and take it down every evening, and her husband will come
out to water the plants. And the people will go up and down
the Steps, and sit out there at night. Everything will go on,
just exactly the same."

"You wouldn't want everything to stop just because you
have to leave it, would you?" Mr. Engel asked reasonably.

"No," said Mrs. Engel, making it a long sound, "not exactly
stop, but be a little different without us. Do you ever——"
She stopped.

"Do I ever what?"

"Well, do you ever feel that when you leave a place you
leave a space behind you, like when something is cut out of a

paper, and that it waits like that until you come back to fill it?"

"No," said Mr. Engel.

"Well, I do," said his wife. "Or else I feel that the person I was while I was there still stays. Like when you pass a house that you used to live in, and you feel that if you went in, you'd find yourself there the way you *used* to be, as if you left little pieces of yourself everywhere you went."

"Well, you do that, all right," said Mr. Engel, "gloves, handkerchiefs, glasses, compacts——"

"I haven't left my glasses anywhere *once*, this whole trip," said Mrs. Engel, interrupting, "at least not to lose them. And anyway, I don't mean things like that." She leaned over the balcony, away from Mr. Engel.

"I know you don't," he said, and leaned with her to watch the shops beginning to sprinkle lights into the warm dusk. "Look," he said, "I don't like leaving either, but we'll be back."

Mrs. Engel said nothing for a moment, and then she straightened. "Anyway," she said, "it isn't as if we were leaving *Italy* tomorrow. There's still Palermo."

"You're still sure you want to leave from there?" Mr. Engel asked, after a moment. "There's time to change your mind if you want to, and we could just get on our ship at Naples, and we'd have a few more days here."

"No," said Mrs. Engel, "ever since we took that trip to Taormina, I've wanted to see more of Sicily, and this way we can. And besides, it won't be so hard to sail from there. I mean, we won't mind so much. It won't be like leaving Rome."

"We'll be leaving Rome wherever we sail from," said Mr. Engel, "and, remember, we have to fly to Palermo, and you know how you are about flying."

"I know," said Mrs. Engel, shutting her eyes briefly, "but if Palermo is anything like Taormina, it'll be worth it. You know how I loved Taormina."

Mr. Engel knew very well how much Mrs. Engel had loved Taormina, and the next afternoon when Rome was behind them and they were on their way from the Palermo airport to their hotel, he wished that Mrs. Engel had been prepared for the fact that Palermo was a city. She said nothing as they were driven to the airport terminal, to transfer to a taxi, nor as they were taken through busy streets that might have been in any city, anywhere, but her silence made Mr. Engel wish that he had been more firm about leaving from Naples.

Then their taxi turned to the waterfront, and the streets were at least wide and open; and after a short while they came to a square with a scattering of houses, and fishermen's huts, and one church, and then they turned into a tree-shaded driveway which wound up a hill to the hotel. As it came into sight Mr. Engel glanced at Mrs. Engel. He knew that she expected something simple and intimate, like a seaside villa. This was a big hotel, tall and spreading, and the lobby was high-ceilinged, and marble-floored, with long echoing halls leading to the public rooms. But it stood high above the harbor, enclosed in formal gardens that flowed colorfully to the sea wall, and, as the porter led the Engels to their room, Mr. Engel felt more hopeful. At first the room seemed gloomy, but when the porter opened the window shutters, there was a tiny balcony outside them, offering sunshine and the scent of the flowers below.

"Kind of a nice view," said Mr. Engel, when the porter had left them. Mrs. Engel nodded. "And there's that little village down the hill," she said, "and a little church. Maybe there'll be something lovely in it like the alabaster madonna in Taormina——" She broke off and looked anxiously at Mr. Engel. "It won't be for long," she said, as if he had demurred. "It's only for a few days."

Mr. Engel lifted Mrs. Engel's dress bag from where the porter had hung it, and put it on a hook that she could reach. "It's going to be fine," he said. "Want to walk down and see the church now?"

"No," said Mrs. Engel. "It's pretty late. Let's just walk around the garden here, and have our cocktail, and dinner earlyish, and start doing things tomorrow." She went out on

the balcony again, and stood looking out at the harbor and the
arm of faraway shore that matched the point on which the
hotel stood.

"It's bigger than Taormina," she said.

The Engels woke early the next morning, and while they
were having breakfast Mrs. Engel went to the balcony and
listened. "It's the church bell," she said, "that means Mass
or something, and the church is sure to be open." She came
back into the room, and some of her old eagerness was back.
"I'll tell you what, I'll just walk down there now, and then
I'll come back and meet you and we can plan the day."

"Will you be all right alone?" asked Mr. Engel.

"It's just at the foot of the drive," said Mrs. Engel. "It's
practically part of the hotel."

"Well, be careful," said Mr. Engel, "watch out for the cars
coming round the turns."

"I'll watch," said Mrs. Engel.

The morning was fresh and cool, and the driveway was
green and shady, and through the shrubs there were glimpses
of the flowers in the garden, and beyond them the glinting
blue of the water. Mrs. Engel thought of the little village just
ahead and quickened her steps. "Maybe it will be like Taormina after all," she said to herself.

But her steps slowed when she left the driveway, and

stopped as she looked around the village. She had expected that it might be poor, but she was unprepared for the bleakness that she found. Although the doors to the low houses were open, she had a feeling that they might as well have been closed, and, although there were trees in its center, the square had a barren look. Close to, the church was shabby and somehow forlorn, and Mrs. Engel thought it looked as though the word "poverty" was written over its pitiful entrance. The square was empty of people, and it occurred to her that perhaps they were all in the church. She hesitated, not liking to intrude on their service, and heard a hissing sound behind her. She turned and saw a child, a girl of perhaps twelve. She wore a stained black calico pinafore, and a piece of worn black net was pinned to her hair. She was thin and sallow, and she looked at Mrs. Engel with a concentrated venom that turned her face to a wizened mask. Wondering, Mrs. Engel put out a tentative hand to her.

"*Poverina*," she said. "*Che cosa?*" It was then that the child spat.

"Actually, it was my fault," Mrs. Engel said, when she had told Mr. Engel about the child. "I had gone down there dressed to go sight-seeing with you. I had gloves on, and a hat, and I looked different from them. Maybe she thought I was showing off, or something. Or patronizing them.

"But the funny thing was," Mrs. Engel continued, as Mr. Engel did not reply, "I wanted to apologize to *her*."

"For what?" Mr. Engel asked.

"I don't know," said Mrs. Engel, "for having more than she had, or whatever it was that made her hate me. I wanted to tell her I couldn't help it, only I didn't know what it was."

Her eyes were bewildered. Hostility had shocked her, Mr. Engel saw, and the trustfulness that he had so often tried to curb had been shaken. Now, he found himself wanting very much to restore it.

"Look," he said, not too surely, "it probably wasn't you she resented, maybe it was some idea she'd been given."

"Maybe," said Mrs. Engel.

"And she was only a child." The shadow on Mrs. Engel's face deepened. "I know," she said. She took her husband's hand and turned it to look at his wrist watch. "Goodness," she said, "if we're going to see the Cathedral and everything, we'd better start." She fingered the watch without looking up. "It's so silly," she said, "I've always wondered why the poor people *didn't* resent us, but now that one did——" She didn't finish.

"It was only a child," Mr. Engel repeated.

"I know," said Mrs. Engel again. She let his hand go and straightened her shoulders. "Well, I'm just going to forget about it, I'm not even going to *think* about it."

But when a taxi had delivered the Engels to the Cathedral,

and they were walking up and down its long, austere aisles, Mr. Engel noticed that though they passed several women who carried babies in their arms, Mrs. Engel did not once stop to admire them.

When they left the Cathedral, they started on foot for a restaurant that the hotel porter had recommended for lunch, and his directions took them into the most crowded part of the city. They were waiting to cross a street, held back by heavy traffic, when, in the midst of the taxis and motor-cycles and bicycles, a flat cart came by, drawn by one white horse. It was an old horse, and behind its blinkers its eyes were stark. It had many scabbed sores, but where the shafts rubbed, the hide was gone completely, and the flesh showed bright and red. There were four men packed on the cart. They were fat and heavy, and it seemed that their weight must drag fresh agony from the open wounds. Mr. Engel pulled Mrs. Engel back, as if to protect her from the cars going by, and tried to stand between her and the horse, but when he took her hand and found it trembling, he knew that she had seen it. She said nothing, and neither did he, but when they were at lunch her face across from him had a pinched look.

"Listen," said Mr. Engel, "would you like to go back to the hotel, and not do anything more today?"

Mrs. Engel put her knife and fork carefully together on her plate. "It wouldn't be fair not to see the nice things," she said.

So, as they had planned earlier, that afternoon the Engels went to the Capella Paletina, and for a moment Mr. Engel saw his wife her old, breathless self. "It's all gold!" she exclaimed. "I didn't know it would be all gold. I never knew mosaics could be like *this!*" It was like a jeweled honeycomb, she thought, that did not so much glitter as glow; as though the light were shining through it, instead of on it.

All the way back to the hotel, she sat quiet in the taxi, and it was only when they passed the village at the foot of the driveway that she spoke. "Poor little church," she said, "I never did go inside it."

With only a short time in Palermo, the Engels could not see everything, but they went to the Cathedral at Monreale, where, again, the mosaics made Mrs. Engel cry out in wonder, and they drove out to a Greek temple that stood in serenity on the green of an ancient hill. Gradually Mrs. Engel began to respond, as she used to, hands outstretched to everything she saw.

It was only with people that she seemed to hang back. The painted carts, that were driven so many long miles to sell a few vegetables at market, delighted her, but she worried about the inevitable panting dogs that trotted underneath them. "I don't see why the drivers don't take them up on the carts," she said, when one went close by. "Why don't you ask them?" Mr. Engel suggested, but immediately she drew into herself. "I don't know enough Italian," she said.

"That never stopped you before," said Mr. Engel, "go ahead and try."

But she shook her head, and although she smiled at Mr. Engel, her eyes worried him. They had clouded over, somehow, he thought, just as they had at the many sharp contrasts that made up Palermo. The modern buildings, the bathing beaches, the wide avenues, and the streets of huddled misery.

It was from a wide avenue that their taxi turned, the afternoon that the Engels went to see a museum of painting. At first they paid little attention to the route, but as it became more and more tortuous, and more and more mean and forbidding, Mrs. Engel took the address she had written down and passed it to the driver, who waved it away. "*Si, si, signora,*" he said, "*E giro.*" He made a whirling gesture with one arm. "*Giro!*" he repeated.

"I guess he means a detour," said Mrs. Engel. "Maybe it'll get better soon."

But the taxi went on through a spider web of streets that deepened into slums, and then it drew up in a *piazza* that seemed to have reached the ultimate in despair. The houses were brown corpses, Mrs. Engel thought, and the washing that hung from every window looked as though it were dying. The air was thick with grit, and outside the houses, women struggled against it with mops and brooms, and on some steps a few old men sat without moving. Near where the taxi stopped, there was a pile of dirt and dust, and four or five ragged children, with blank eyes, played there, as if it were a sand pile.

"Where are we?" Mr. Engel asked.

"I don't know," said Mrs. Engel.

"Should we get out?"

"I don't know," Mrs. Engel said again. Her eyes, Mr. Engel noticed, had gone to the children.

The taxi driver was holding the cab door open, and beckoning. "No," said Mrs. Engel, *"non e museo."*

The driver was voluble in Italian, and pointed to a nearby alley, then, as Mrs. Engel did not understand him, he slowed his speech. *"Museo,"* he said, pointing again. *"Prego, signora, non abbiate paura. Sono poveri, ma non cattivi."*

"What did he say?" Mr. Engel asked.

"I'm not sure," Mrs. Engel answered. "I think he said 'poor but not bad.' I think he means the people here."

Slowly she got out of the taxi, and, not looking at the children, let the taxi driver lead herself and Mr. Engel down the alley to a street that was an eviscerated ditch. The driver gave his hand to Mrs. Engel and helped her to avoid the exposed drainpipes, then brought her to where a low, handsome building was set well back from the street. *"Museo!"* he cried triumphantly. Inside, the museum was light and cool, a world so

far removed from its surroundings that the beauty that blazed
on its walls came almost as a shock to the Engels. But their
taxi driver, who had followed them in, stood looking at it, the
way, Mrs. Engel thought, a man who has been cold stands in
front of an open fire.

When they left the museum, the street outside seemed more
than ever wretched, and the *piazza*, when they reached it,
more miserable and squalid. The children still crawled on the
pile of dust, and though Mrs. Engel passed close to them,
they did not look up, but went on playing as they had before,
without sound or laughter.

"Too many," said Mrs. Engel, when the cab had started
away.

"Too many what?" asked Mr. Engel.

"Children," she said. "They can't take care of them."

Time was running out. The Engels drove up a mountain
road whose smooth new macadam led to an ancient shrine,
where pink wax replicas of arms and legs and other anatomical
features hung in testimony of miraculous cures. They drove
through a huge park, and Mrs. Engel was happier in the tiny
garden that lay behind a church in the city; a tiny, flowering
cloister, with peace at its heart, brooded over by red-pink
domes that made her think of strawberry ice cream.

They stopped at a square where a large painted canvas was drawn across one side, and lights were strung, ready to be lit.

"It's a *festa*," Mrs. Engel said. "Maybe we'll be here for it!" But when she examined the canvas, it was a call to a political rally, and the figures painted on it were bloated men in Roman togas, and the men were driving chariots drawn by workers in modern clothes. "Goodness," Mrs. Engel said, "even if they feel that way, you'd think they'd have the periods *match*."

They had dinner at a restaurant where silent men and women were handed newspaper parcels over the outside hedge. "Food to take out?" Mr. Engel asked. "I don't think so," Mrs. Engel answered. "I think they're just giving it to them."

They drove to another restaurant that hung on a cliff, its clear glass windows and outer terrace looking down on what could have been the whole of Sicily. The bay spread out and out, and there were rocks that might have held the Sirens.

"*Molto bello*," said Mr. Engel, quoting Mrs. Engel's constant expression in Rome. "*Molto*," she said. "Only——"

"Only what?"

"Just those houses in that village as we came through, driving here. It's so *open* here, and they looked so close together, and so dark."

On the way back, they passed through the village again, and every door to every house stood open, to show a lighted room, and in each room was a table with a bright cloth, and on each table was a vase of flowers. From every upper window, pieces of silk and damask hung, worn and unhemmed, but brave with color. There were people leaning from the windows and lining the street, and from the church a procession was starting. Boys and girls carrying lighted candles, and acolytes holding a silk canopy over a vestmented priest.

The Engels stopped the car to watch. "It's as though they were all expecting a guest," Mrs. Engel said, looking at the open doors. "Is the priest going to visit the houses?"

"I don't know," said Mr. Engel, but this time he did not suggest that Mrs. Engel ask anyone else.

As they drove away, she looked back. "The houses aren't really dark, when you see them this way," she said. "They look sort of proud."

The Engels' last day in Palermo was a Sunday, and they planned to go to Monreale again. But first Mrs. Engel wanted to stop at a Byzantine church that had been closed when they had gone before. They took a taxi from the hotel, and reached the church at a time when no Mass was being said. But the church was unexceptional. It was not what Mrs. Engel had hoped it would be and she was about to leave when a group of festively dressed Sicilians came up the aisle and went to the altar rail, and stood waiting expectantly. "Maybe it's a wedding," said Mrs. Engel. "Let's stay and watch."

"Perhaps it's private," said Mr. Engel.

"I don't think anything is private in Italy," said Mrs. Engel. "Let's wait."

She and Mr. Engel stood a little to one side, and soon a bearded priest came and took his place, just outside the altar rail; then from the back of the church came two or three women and a young man carrying a baby in his arms.

"It's a *christening*," Mrs. Engel whispered. "Another baby!" The young man went to the priest, and the priest met him and walked with him to the foot of the aisle, the others following. Some of them had lighted candles in their hands now, and they held them in a circle where the priest halted. If there was a font, Mrs. Engel did not see it. She thought that an acolyte held the baptismal water in a silver basin, but she wasn't sure because she was watching the face of the young man who held the baby. He had none of the self-consciousness of the young father. He was grave and concentrated and there was a dedication in his look, which was reflected in the faces around him. The lit candles brought them into relief, and their seriousness gave them beauty. They were like one of the paintings from the museum, Mrs. Engel thought, come suddenly to life. The priest spoke the words of baptism, and, as he made the sign of the cross on the baby's forehead, the baby put up one exploring hand to the ancient one, and for a second it was as though there were a compact between them. The old priest smiled, and the watching women caught their breath, and then the ceremony was over, and the young man walked back with the priest to the altar, holding the baby out from him on his spread hands and looking down at it, as if it were a miracle.

When the Engels left the church, Mr. Engel saw Mrs. Engel fumbling futilely in her handbag. "Here," he said, and gave her his handkerchief.

Their taxi was waiting for them, their driver holding open the door. "Monreale, *per favore*," Mrs. Engel told him, and he shut the door on them, and got into his own seat, and started the engine. With that, a strange man swung himself into the other front seat, and the cab started off. The stranger was squat and swart, and Mrs. Engel thought he looked like a secure spider.

"Who's this?" asked Mr. Engel.

"I don't know," said Mrs. Engel.

"Ought we to find out?"

Mrs. Engel did not reply, and Mr. Engel turned to her. She was clinging to the strap on her side, and sitting forward. It wasn't like her, Mr. Engel thought, and any misgiving he felt himself, he decided to conceal.

"It's probably a friend, getting a lift," he said.

"Yes," said Mrs. Engel. Something about her made Mr. Engel feel uneasy, and he tried to make a joke of it for her.

"Maybe we're being kidnaped," he said. "Aren't there bandits in Sicily?" The reaction he expected did not come. Instead of her usual hot denial of any suspicion on his part, she clung tighter to the strap and sat more forward.

"Look," said Mr. Engel, "want to tell him to go back to the hotel, or let us out here?"

At that, Mrs. Engel loosened her grip on the strap, and made a movement as if she were shaking something off.

"Of course not, dear, that would be silly when we want to see the mosaics again. And the view of the valley," she said in what her husband recognized as her social voice. "It was misty when we went before. Today it ought to be wonderful."

They drove along, and Mrs. Engel kept her eyes on the road. "This *is* the way we came before," she said once, as much to herself as to Mr. Engel.

Presently they reached Monreale, and stopped in front of the Cathedral. The Square was gay with people in their Sunday best, strolling and chatting. There were postcard sellers, flower sellers and candy sellers; churchgoers, and camera-strung tourists, and the sun poured down on them like a benediction.

Their driver helped the Engels out of the cab, and Mrs.

Engel thanked him, glancing back to the spider sitting silent in the front seat. She waited a moment, and then turned and went with Mr. Engel toward the Cathedral and the mosaics within.

The High Mass had just finished, and the Engels stood to watch the last moments of the procession from the High Altar. When it was over, and the last note of the Recessional, the last drift of incense, had trailed to nothingness, and the throng of worshipers had poured itself into the sunlit Square, Mr. and Mrs. Engel sat down and looked a long time at the glory made from infinitesimal fragments of gold and colored stone, put together by the myriad patient hands of men centuries dead.

The Engels walked by the side altars, and came to one where a silk-robed madonna looked down on rows of twinkling candles. Mr. Engel waited. He knew Mrs. Engel's theory about lighting candles in the churches they visited. "I do it because I'm *not* a Catholic," she had told him, and, although he did not completely understand her reasoning, he believed it had something to do with being polite, and so now he stood aside to let her approach the glittering stand, she only stood a moment, and went on to the next altar. Mr. Engel started to follow, and then went to the stand himself.

"Where were you?" his wife asked, when he caught up with her.

"Nowhere," said Mr. Engel. "I was right here."

They went out to the cloisters, and then, finally, to the narrow park behind them to look once more over its railing to the splendor of the Conco D'Oro below.

The park was full of people, visitors and townspeople. As the Engels stood by the railing, a family passed. Three or four adults, and a little girl that Mr. Engel thought was the most exquisite he had ever seen. She wore the long, full muslin dress of First Communion, and her face was a delicate ivory under a white wreath. She walked with the dignity of a young princess, and her parents walked a pace behind her, as though they hardly dared to claim her solemn beauty.

Mr. Engel touched Mrs. Engel's arm. She would go straight to the child, he was sure, and pour out her few Italian words of delight and compliment. He waited, but she only took one indecisive step forward, and then drew back. Mr. Engel was not an imaginative man, but at that moment he saw another figure come between Mrs. Engel and the white-clad Sicilian infanta, a child in a stained black pinafore, hissing and hostile.

Mrs. Engel turned again to the railing, and gazed out at the incredible view.

"We couldn't have not come, could we?" she said. "We had to *try* to see it again."

"Well, sure," said Mr. Engel. "I just thought you didn't like that guy riding in the front seat."

As they walked back to the Square, Mrs. Engel caught Mr. Engel's arm.

"Look," she said, "whatever happens, just say '*non capisco.*'"

"What's *that?*" Mr. Engel said.

"'I don't understand,'" Mrs. Engel translated for him. "It's always the safest thing to say."

She took her hand from his arm, and went briskly to the taxi. The driver was waiting for them, and the spider was gone.

Mrs. Engel started to get into the taxi, and halted. On the seat inside was a bunch of crimson carnations, a little sparse, but fresh and fragrant.

The driver struggled to explain. "My *amico,*" he said, pointing to where the spider had sat, "he give *Signora,* for tell *grazie* for *gentilezza! Gratzie* for lift."

On the way back to Palermo, Mr. Engel sighed. "I *gave* you my handkerchief," he said. "Look in your bag."

Mrs. Engel looked in her bag, and found it.

"It's just that I've been so *awful,*" she said. "I truly thought he was going to hold us up. Even in the Cathedral, in front of that *altar,* I was thinking they would take us off on a side road on the way back, and hold us up, or something." She blew her nose, wetly. "It's just that everything's been so mixed up here. That poor old horse, and those awful men driving it, and the hotel, and the restaurants, and right beside them people with no food at all. And the big beaches, and then those children making castles in a dirt pile. And you think there are too many children, and then they looked at that baby this morning as if it were the only one that had ever been born." She blew her nose again. "And I wanted to speak to that little girl in the park just now, but I was afraid. I've been just awful," she repeated damply, "but it's so difficult. I was sorry for that little girl in the village, and she spat at me, and I was suspicious of that poor man who rode out with us. I was *scared* of him, and he gave me flowers. I don't know *what* to think."

"Think of the flowers," said Mr. Engel. Mrs. Engel touched the carnations. "He probably couldn't even afford them," she said.

"Well," said Mr. Engel. "Think of that, too."

Later that evening, when the Engels were in the outdoor bar of their hotel, having their last cocktails in Italy, Mrs. Engel spoke.

"I guess maybe it's like the mosaics," she said.

"What is?" asked Mr. Engel.

"What I was talking about in the taxi," she answered. "Everything that we've seen here, and maybe everywhere we've been. You know how when you stand close to the mosaics, they're just little bits of stones all stuck together, and they seem to make no sense, but when you stand away from them, they come together and make a picture that you can understand? Well, maybe when we're far enough away, maybe when we're home, we'll understand all this."

"Maybe," said Mr. Engel.

The harbor was darkening in the failing light. A boat went out, slim and white on the sapphire water. Rowboats full of young people were passing close to the hotel, returning to the village at its foot. As they rowed they sang, and their voices lingered, clear and happy.

"They're going back to nothing," Mrs. Engel thought, "but they go singing." She thought back over the morning, and of the red carnations in a vase on her dressing table upstairs in the hotel. "I'll take them to the ship, tomorrow," she decided, "and if it has a chapel, I'll put them there."

Something came to her mind, then, and she turned to Mr. Engel.

"Where were you really," she said, "when I missed you in the Cathedral?"

"I wasn't anywhere," said Mr. Engel.

"You were *somewhere*," said Mrs. Engel. "It was two or three minutes, and you weren't with *me*."

"I went back to light a candle," said Mr. Engel, and signaled the waiter. "I'd like another cocktail," he said to Mrs. Engel, "how about you?"

"I'd love another," she said.

While it was being made, she thought of Mr. Engel going back to light a candle, the candle that she had omitted. She was pretty sure that was why he had done it, though it might have been for some other reason. He would never tell her, she knew, and she would never ask. She would just remember it. It was sort of like another stone in a mosaic, she thought, only a small mosaic, and different from the others, because this one was her own, and this one you had to be close to, to understand.

Ladies to the Center

VIEW FROM A CLOSED WINDOW

*D*une View, referred to by its owner, Mrs. Farleigh, as a cottage, was in reality a substantial ten-room house built in the gray-shingled tradition of the Island on which it stood. Its old-fashioned exterior sheltered the most modern of bathrooms and kitchens and every other adjunct to comfortable living, all, however, artfully subservient to a calculated simplicity of decoration. Unpainted wicker chairs creaked in the wide, wood-walled living room, and the English chintz of the curtains and cushions was sufficiently worn to support Mrs. Farleigh's references to her dear shabby room. That the room was dear to her was true, but less for its shabbiness than its casement window that looked squarely out to the ocean and from which she could enjoy the sensation of being on the beach without any of the discomforts of sand or flies or wind. The narrow dirt road on which Dune View stood was as yet unspoiled by any of the improvements that Mrs. Farleigh fought yearly at Town Meetings, and remained a narrow dirt road running along the steep bank that fell to the expanse of dunes which in turn led to the sea. Only a few feet of trim grass separated the house from the road, and when no one was actually walking past, Mrs. Farleigh had a feeling of command over the blue and green and gold sweep beyond her window which was ordinarily very soothing to her. Today, though, there was a cold look in her handsome eyes, and a furrow of distaste on her otherwise unlined forehead. She rose from her chair and stood looking down to where a fat, year-old boy scrabbled in a sandbox with a toy spade. Beside him a young girl lay flat on her stomach, her legs ungracefully spread, her chin propped on her folded arms. She had a round, sunburned face and untidy red hair pulled into a desultory pony-tail, and she was watching the baby's aimless pattings and scrapings as if they were the most fascinating game in the world.

"Look at her," said Mrs. Farleigh to her daughter who sat near the fireplace, bent hooplike over a novel. "I ask you to look at her."

"Who, Mother?" said the younger woman without looking up.

" 'Who, Mother,' " said Mrs. Farleigh, imitating her daughter's disinterest. "Really, Gloria, sometimes I think you're not quite bright. That girl in charge of your son. That nursemaid, if that's what you call her."

"Margaret? What's wrong with her?"

"What's wrong with her? If you'd get out of that chair for five minutes and take your nose out of those eternal books occasionally, you might have some idea of what is wrong with her. Of course I realize you are pregnant again and that you have to take things easily, and leave everything for your mother to do for you, I realize that——"

"I know, you've been wonderful, Mother," said her daughter, her eyes still following the page of her book.

"Well, it's not that I'm not glad to help you—what else have I to live for now, with your father gone—but if I am to help you, the least you might do is look at what I have to cope with.

"All right, Mother," said the younger woman wearily. She dragged her awkward heaviness out of the low chair and went to look down at the two on the grass. "What's the matter?" she asked. "They look all right." "They!" said Mrs. Farleigh. "Of course *he* looks all right, the blessed lamb—was he a beauty, was he a precious *boy*——" she murmured, waving down to the baby. "Poor little thing," she added, half under her breath. "What is it, Mother?" her daughter asked. "I don't see anything wrong." Mrs. Farleigh sniffed. "Have you looked at your nursemaid?" she asked in return. "Well," said her daughter, "what's wrong with *her?*" "Bare feet," said Mrs. Farleigh. "Bare feet in front of the *house*. And shorts. She's wearing shorts now, if you please." Her daughter stared at her. "Well, for heaven's sake, Mother, what if she is? I don't say it isn't a mistake with her legs, but she's happy and comfortable, and she's wonderful with the baby, so what else matters?" She watched her son for a moment or two and then tapped on the window for his attention. "My darling!" she mouthed to him, her thin face made beautiful by the words. The girl in shorts said something inaudible through the glass. Mrs. Farleigh threw open the window with a decisive movement and her hair blew in the wind that she disliked. "I said he was building a house, a little house," the girl called happily. "Well, it's getting too hot for him out there now," said Mrs. Farleigh. "You can bring him in, and I want to speak to you, please." "Mother," said her daughter. Mrs. Farleigh closed the window and pushed her hair into place again. "It is perfect nonsense," she said. "She has a perfectly good uniform that I bought her myself, and if you have no regard for appearances I have. She came here to work and she is behaving as if she were on a holiday; she acts like it, and she dresses like it!"

"It is a sort of holiday for her, I think," said Mrs. Farleigh's daughter. "She's never been off the mainland before. I don't think she has ever been out of the Home before."

"The Home! I said it was a mistake then, and I say it again now. When you take a girl from a place like that you don't know what you are letting yourself in for. If you had listened to me——"

"Mother," said the younger woman, interrupting, "the Home is all right, it isn't a fallen women thing, you know, and anyway there just aren't any nursemaids, the kind you're thinking of, any more."

"Nonsense. There are still plenty of children's nurses to be had, good, responsible, well-trained women."

"Mother," said the younger woman patiently, "if there were thousands of them lined up screaming for the job, George and I couldn't afford anyone like that." Mrs. Farleigh said nothing. "George does everything he can for me," her daughter

said, interpreting the silence, "but with this other baby coming——"

"Well, you know what I think about that," said Mrs. Farleigh, "so we won't discuss it, but if you had left the nurse to
me, I was, and still am, ready to make it my responsibility."

"Please, Mother," said her daughter, "George wants to do
these things himself. We both do. But don't worry, I'll speak
to Margaret, and I'll see that she wears her uniform." "And
shoes," said Mrs. Farleigh. "And shoes," said her daughter,
turning to leave the room. "And tell her to sit properly out
there with the baby," Mrs. Farleigh said as she went, "and not
sprawl all over the grass as if she lived here!"

For the next two days Margaret wore her uniform and took
a campstool to sit on when she watched the baby; once Mrs.
Farleigh saw that she had turned the stool on its side and was
making some kind of game for the baby with it. "Here's the
little door," Mrs. Farleigh heard her say, "and here's the little
room with the tea all ready." Mrs. Farleigh shrugged. At least
the girl was sitting upright on the grass and not sprawling, and
she was wearing well-whitened canvas shoes, although her
sturdy, reddened legs were unstockinged. Why was it girls
like that always had mosquito bites, Mrs. Farleigh wondered
irritably, and scratched them.

It was on the third day that she looked up from where she
was sewing in the window, startled by an unaccustomed sound.

Margaret was coming toward the front steps, on her way back from the post office. She had a postcard and a straggly bunch of wildflowers in one hand, and the other swung a parcel carelessly by its string. Her uniform sleeves were rolled lumpily to her shoulders, and she was whistling. Mrs. Farleigh closed her eyes until the whistling stopped, and opened them to see Margaret standing just inside the room.

"Oh, it's you, Margaret," Mrs. Farleigh said. "I couldn't think who it could be, whistling and stamping up the steps like that."

"It was me," said Margaret. "I got the mail and there's a parcel came. I don't know what's in it, though. It's for your daughter." Mrs. Farleigh winced. "Well, if it's for Mrs. Gordon," she said, "put it on the table for her. Not the small table, Margaret, the big table. The big one, Margaret." She sighed. "Was the mail late?" she asked then. "You were gone quite a while, weren't you?"

"I walked back by the houses," said the girl, her round face alight.

"I don't quite see how you could do anything else, there are nothing but houses from here to the post office."

"I mean the little houses," said the girl, "the little ones in a row over in the back of the big ones."

Mrs. Farleigh took a stitch in her sewing. She must mean the Artists' Colony, she thought, not that there were any artists there. What few artists came to the Island maintained large houses, larger than Mrs. Farleigh's, where they lived decorously and formally. The so-called Colony was a cluster of the merest huts; rose-covered, inconvenient, surprisingly expensive, but enthusiastically rented by single ladies with a passion for the picturesque. "Surely you have seen them before?" Mrs. Farleigh said to the girl, who answered eagerly.

"Oh, I have, but only driving by in the car with your daughter. I wanted to walk past them slow."

"Well, I'm sure that was very gratifying, but hardly very thoughtful. Perhaps it didn't occur to you that I might be anxious for my letters?"

"Oh, it did indeed," said the girl, "but there wasn't any letter, only the postcard and the parcel, and they weren't for you at all." Mrs. Farleigh put down her sewing and looked at the girl. "That will do, Margaret," she said. "Another time be more considerate, please. And I think you will find your uniform more comfortable if you wear the sleeves nicely buttoned down as they should be. At the moment you look as if you were about to embark on a day's washing." She smiled as if she had meant a pleasantry, and the girl smiled back, uncertainly. "Oh, and Margaret," Mrs. Farleigh continued, "don't bring those weeds you have picked anywhere near my grandson, will you? We have to think of allergies, don't we?"

"Yes, ma'am," said the girl, flushing.

She left the room and went slowly up the stairs to the room where she slept with the baby. He was out with his mother, for once, and she had it to herself for a while. It wasn't often she was alone in the room, she thought, and when she was she liked to have something nice to think about to herself, not like this minute when she'd give a lot to sit down and cry after the way Mrs. Farleigh had talked to her, making her feel all arms and legs. She hadn't meant to keep her waiting, something had told her to hurry back like always, but she had wanted to walk by the little houses. They were so little and snug a person could live in one by herself and never be a bit alone. It was the little house that kept a person safe and contented when you came down to it. The big houses were too roomy altogether, you'd need a lot of people coming and going to make them friendly, and where would be the coziness then? There were people coming and going in the Home, and the nuns everywhere, and the other girls all around you all day and all night, and they were kind, and friendly as much as they could be, but it was a lonely thing being with people forever, and everything so big. Big refectories, big dormitories, big long halls and never a small place to go to. It was a small place she thought she was coming to here, when Reverend Mother told her she had a summer job for her, "a summer cottage," she'd said, but it was a big house with a cook and all, and that was Mrs. Farleigh all over, letting on that she had everything plain when a cat could see it wasn't so. She was a hard one to please, whatever you did. The young one was different entirely, as easy as an old shoe. Hadn't they had a grand time together coming over to the Island, herself and the baby and the young one in the little room on the boat. A stateroom they called it, but it was as good as a little house, with chairs and a sofa and a door you could shut. It wasn't till Mrs. Farleigh got the whiphand of them all that she hadn't felt on wings to be out of the Home and have the sea everywhere and the wind to blow on her. Still and all, she thought, wasn't that a wonderful thing in itself, and hadn't she a room with no one but the baby in it? If she shut her eyes, she needn't see his crib or his playpen, or all the other things of his that filled the room to the corners. She could shut her eyes now and hear no one in the room but herself breathing, and till the baby came back it was like her own little place. If she had only the young one to please, she thought, she could stay on after the summer till the new little baby came, and get to be one of those family nurses and stay on and on till one day she'd have a room to herself, maybe. That would be a grand thing, she thought, and if she'd watch out from now on, and not annoy the old lady, please God she'd not have to go back to the big Home, but have some place cozy and small in the end.

She got up from her bed where she had been sitting, and smoothed it to convent neatness. The flowers she had picked drooped where she had dropped them. "Not near my grand-son," Mrs. Farleigh had said. "Well, then, I'll throw them away," she said to herself, "but I'll give them a drink of water first, the creatures." She went to the bathroom to run water into the drinking glass there, and saw herself in the mirror over the basin. "I'm a wild-looking thing," she thought, "with my hair all anyway, and my sleeves rolled up on me, and Reverend Mother would murder me if she saw me. Sure, the old one had a right to be mad with me." She filled the glass carefully and put the limp wild roses in it, and looked at her reflection again. She pulled down her sleeves, but they were crumpled from the rolling, and looked no better. "The long sleeves are a nuisance, altogether, with all I have to do for the baby," she thought, "and the nylon is suffocating in the heat. If I cut the sleeves short, now, and hemmed them nicely, they'd be cool and tidy and they wouldn't crush on me. And I'll plait my hair in a bun, unless I cut it short, too. That way I'll be neat always." She smiled at the round red face in the mirror and it seemed to smile back at her. "That's the way," it seemed to say, "keep on like that, Margaret Reilly, and one of these days you'll be safe."

A week later Mrs. Farleigh sat contentedly at her window, looking out at the long and lovely line of blue that marked the ocean beyond the dunes. On the grass outside, a solidly built woman, circumspect in white linen, sat knitting in a deck chair, glancing down now and then at the child dabbling in the sandbox at her feet. Anyone passing could see that here was a well-regulated household, unostentatious but solid and serene. "You see," Mrs. Farleigh said to her daughter, who was reading in her usual place. "It can be done." "M'm," murmured her daughter from the page she was intent on. "When I think of what we put up with from that girl," Mrs. Farleigh said. Her daughter moved in her chair but made no answer.

"You know, really," said Mrs. Farleigh, taking up her sewing, "I think she was feeble-minded, I really do. I put up with her sprawling and whistling and dawdling and leaving weeds in the baby's bathroom, but the uniform was the last straw. That good uniform that cost sixteen dollars. Hacked to pieces!"

"She only shortened the sleeves," said the younger woman from her book.

"Hacked or shortened, no respect is what it amounted to. No respect for people or property or anything else."

"Well, she's gone," said the younger woman.

"Indeed she has and in short order. If I had left it to you she'd still be here, thank you. But I took one look at her and I called the Home, and then I contacted Nurse Williamson and gave Miss Margaret her walking papers." Mrs. Farleigh pricked a finger and sucked it. "I tell you," she went on, "I think she was feeble-minded. Cutting off her hair and looking wilder than ever! But at least that was her loss, it didn't cost me sixteen dollars." The younger woman turned a page of her book. "And I told you what she said when I paid her for you, and gave her her ticket for the boat?" "Yes, Mother, you did," said the reading girl.

"But I can't get over it. How would she go about getting a stateroom on the boat, she asked me. A stateroom, Margaret, I said, do you know what staterooms cost? She said no, but she wanted one. I said to her, Margaret, my daughter had one coming here because she isn't well, and you were in it with her to take care of the baby, but by yourself, for a few hours to the mainland, what do you want of such a thing, I asked her, and what do you think she said?"

"You told me," said the younger woman.

"I know, but I can't yet make any sense out of it. 'I want one of the little houses,' she said, 'I want one of the little houses on the boat. I can be in it by myself for the little time till I get back.' Do *you* know what she was talking about?"

"No, Mother," said Mrs. Farleigh's daughter.

"And neither do I," said Mrs. Farleigh, "and, if you ask me, neither did she. Little house!" she repeated on a breath, "little crazy!" She looked out of her window and down to the placid scene on the grass below it, and then let her eyes go to the dunes and sea. "It's lovely out there today," she said, returning to her sewing, "quite lovely."

𝒥t was after five, and the department-store powder room was almost empty. Women were gathering their handbags and small parcels and scurrying out on their way to trains and buses. The maid was washing out the basins and picking up towels; as she went back and forth, she eyed the blond woman who sat at the long mirrored shelf, an assortment of cosmetics spread before her. Deliberately, unhurriedly, she was making herself a new face. Pink cream rouge well rubbed in. Pinkish powder patted smooth. Blue eyeshadow on and over the heavy lids. Dry rouge over the powder. Even in the artificial light the colors were vivid; in the lingering daylight outside they would be garish, but slowly, intently, she continued to apply them. Her harsh, yellow hair had a freshly done look, and her hat, which she had not removed, looked brand-new. It had pink water lilies on it, like floral ear muffs, and it was made of green felt—a bright green, as hard and penetrating as a scream. Her nails were magenta stubs.

The maid passed again and looked at the clock significantly.

Behind the woman stood a young girl. She was fair, too, but beside the gold and carmine of the older woman her fairness looked gray. Her eyes were gray, and they watched the process at the mirror with patience.

The woman glanced past her own reflection to the girl's.

"Listen, Babette," she said. "Don't you want to go home?" The girl answered the reflection in the mirror. "No, Mother," she said.

The woman went back to her task. She took a brown pencil and traced her eyebrows over and over until they were even and exact, their last naturalness gone. "Because I don't need you," she said. "We done all the shopping and all, and it won't be any fun for you hanging around."

The girl said nothing.

"Whyn't you go home," the woman repeated. "And I'll be out on the seven-ten."

"It's all right, Mother," the girl said. "I don't mind staying in."

The woman genteely moistened a finger and transferred the wetness to the mascara. Then she brushed her eyelashes till they stood out and up, stickily black. "Aren't you tired?" she asked then. "I should think you'd be tired," she said. "You *look* tired."

The girl shook her head. "I'm not tired," she said.

"Whyn't you sit down?" the woman said. "You don't need to stand like that. Whyn't you sit down?"

"I'm all right," said the girl.

"Sit down," said her mother. "I want to talk to you, anyways."

The girl sat down, almost without movement.

The woman peered at herself in the mirror. "Listen, Babette," she said. "It's been on my mind all day. I don't want you to mention names in public like you did."

"When did I?"

"When we met those persons today, you did. You mentioned

that other person we met's name. And you mentioned it to me in here, too. It's not nice to mention names in public places, no matter where it is."

"What did I say?" asked the girl.

"You didn't say anything," said her mother, "but you mentioned that person's name, and there might be someone that knew them and they'd say, 'Oh, I heard your name mentioned the other day.' And anyways, I don't like you to mention names in public places."

"All right," said the girl. "I'll be careful."

"There's nothing to be careful about," the woman said. "It just isn't nice."

"I won't any more."

"That's right, dear."

The woman straightened a little, as if the rebuke had re-established an authority, and she applied an orange lipstick lavishly. Then she took a small mirror and examined her face from every angle. She settled the water lilies closer to her ears, careful not to disturb a single stiff wave of hair. Then she put down the glass and turned to face her daughter for the first time. "Babette!" she exclaimed. "You know what, dear? You haven't eaten yet. You should have got you a sandwich while I was having my set. You must be starving!"

The girl smiled faintly, but her look was steady.

Her mother met it, and then seemed to retreat. "But I suppose you don't mind," she said evenly.

"No, Mother," the girl said. "I don't mind."

The woman began to put her things together. One by one the pencils and boxes went into her shiny green bag. She snapped it shut and rose, brushing powder from the breast of her checked suit. She swung a fur piece over her shoulders and put on a pair of bright-green gloves. They were new, and she had to break the little thread that held them together. Then she stood perfectly still, looking herself over from head to foot, without joy or pleasure, but seriously and carefully, as a mechanic might check an engine before a flight.

She went to the door marked "Out" and then turned. "Listen, Babette," she said. "You're sure you don't want to go on home? It's just this girl I used to know that I haven't seen since she was married, like I told you. There won't be no one for you. You ought to get your food, anyways. You and your father can go to the movies, maybe. I'll be out on the seven-ten, or the eight-twenty-one at the latest."

The girl said nothing but very gently pushed open the door and waited for her mother to pass. Their eyes met again, and held, and then the woman's checked shoulders suddenly sagged.

"All right," she said. "Come on then. I guess we can make the six-five." She went out, walking a little gingerly on her spike-heeled shoes. Her legs were thin for her body, but shapely, and her pleated skirt barely covered her knees.

The girl followed her mother, and as she went, she tugged at her own skirt, as if to lengthen it.

She was of medium age and height, and the few strands of hair that blew from under her gay head scarf were medium brown. Her eyes were brown, too, bright and alert, and her manner was eager. She smiled at me across the sundeck, and then came and sat on the foot of the deck chair next to mine, and clasped her hands over the small, expensive-looking camera that hung from a strap round her neck, like a talisman. I knew her by sight as a member of a mixed group of eight that was traveling together happily, if a little noisily, but this was the first time that she had spoken to me.

"Don't tell them I was taking their pictures, will you?" she murmured anxiously, jerking her head toward a couple that was sprawled on the edge of the pool, taking blissful advantage of the sun which, now that we were approaching the Azores, had at last come out from the clouds that had persisted all the way from New York. I had not noticed any picture-taking, and, in any case, the chance of my acting as informer was slight, but I indicated that my lips were sealed.

"Well, thanks," she said with relief, "because it's for Christmas."

I had been lying in my chair, just touching sleep, thinking hazily of the March blizzard in which we had sailed, and looking forward to the long European spring and summer still ahead for me, so that Christmas seemed not only remote but improbable. I must have looked startled, because the woman laughed.

"I guess you think that's planning pretty far off," she said, "but we have this cute little game, my husband and me. We take snaps of our friends, like on this trip or at home, and then at Christmas, instead of sending pictures of ourselves or our children for Christmas cards, we send everyone pictures of *them*selves. They've forgotten by then that we took them, if they ever knew we did, so it's a cute surprise." She pushed a brown curl back under her scarf which had I LOVE YOU printed on it in several languages. "It's so hard to find anything personal for Christmas cards that isn't your home or your family, so these are a real change for everybody. I think Christmas cards are awful these days. The kind you buy, they're all so commercial, and my husband said one year he'd rather send none at all than something that wasn't personal, and that's when we got this idea of taking pictures of people. People we know, of course."

"Of course," I said.

"And cute, like the ones I just took." She giggled. "It'll come out mostly their feet, and I'll write something on it like 'hang your Christmas presents here,' as if they were Christmas trees, or maybe 'hang your Christmas *stockings* here,' anyway something cute like that, because I think Christmas cards ought to be cute as well as personal." She wriggled. "I'll tell you though," she said, "some friends of ours had a *really* cute idea for Christmas cards, once. It took me three years to catch on. Three *years!*"

I said consolingly that I wasn't very good at puzzles, either.

"It wasn't a puzzle the way you mean," she said. "It was a

continued card, sort of. The year the first one came, I couldn't think *what* it was. It was this picture of the whole family in bed together. No explanation—nothing. Just 'the night before Christmas' written on it in red ink. Not printed or anything, just written."

I nodded to show that I understood.

"Well," she said, "even the night before Christmas I couldn't see why they'd all be together in one bed—I mean all of them were, the children and all—so I just put it away and forgot it, and then next year there was another of them!"

"Still in bed?" I asked.

"No," she said, "at least, the children were, but May and Eddie—that's our friends' names that sent it—were sort of looking out of a window, and it still said 'the night before Christmas,' and the next year they were sort of listening to something, and finally I caught on. Do you know what it was?"

I shook my head.

"It was the poem," she said, "it was the poem about the night before Christmas, and they were acting it out in pictures! Don't you think that was cute?"

I delayed too long in answering, and the spark of topaz that excitement had brought to her brown eyes faded.

"You don't," she said flatly. "You *don't* think it's cute."

I tried to make amends. I said that perhaps it seemed a bit prolonged, and a great deal of work. She considered this.

"Oh, it was a lot of work, all right, and of course they were taking chances. I mean, if one of them had died or anything, it would have spoiled the whole thing. But I still think it was cute."

She sounded so wistful that I told her that at least I thought it was unusual.

"That's it," she agreed, looking happier, "and it's so hard to find unusual Christmas cards. Don't you just get sick of the whole thing, sometimes?"

I had to admit that I rather liked looking for Christmas cards. To be more amenable, I said that I liked sending them, and that I *loved* getting them.

She studied me for a moment.

"What kind do you send?" she asked.

I said that I usually sent something that had to do with Christmas.

"Christmas?" she said vaguely.

"I mean," I explained apologetically, "something that has to do with what Christmas is *about*. Sort of," I added, hoping to sound less sententious.

"Oh," she said, after a delay of her own. "Traditional. Well, of course you can always get *those*."

She rose, inclined her head briefly, and left me.

I pulled my steamer rug to my nose and sought sleep again, but found my mind immediately involved with the problems of a large family solemnly planning a series of pictures that from year to year would baffle their friends. Did they do the whole poem in one concentrated sitting? No, because the children would have to have grown each time, and there might even be new ones. Who took the group pictures, if it was all to be a surprise? Not a friend, because then he wouldn't be surprised. Father himself, with a string tied to the shutter? The local photographer, smuggled in disguised as a plumber?

I turned restlessly under my rug, and came face to face with St. Nicholas. Who posed for *him*, I wondered. Grandfather, probably, or, in a pinch, Gram. And how about the reindeer? Did the family pets oblige? An array of dogs, cats, and hamsters swirled under my closed lids, and I opened my eyes to dispel it and saw that my new acquaintance was back. She was standing in front of me, her camera in her hands.

"I didn't take you," she said, as I began a weak protest. "I could have, but I wouldn't unless I knew you better. No—what it is, I want to tell you something. You know what you said about traditional?"

It had been her word, but I accepted it.

"Well, you've given me an idea. I guess you know there are eight of us taking this trip? Well, when the boys are playing bridge together tonight, I'm going to sneak a picture of them, and I'll send it out next Christmas, and I'll call it 'The Three Wise Men.' What do you think of that?"

I peered up at her fuzzily. "If they're playing bridge, won't they have to be the *four* wise men?" I asked.

"No, she said—and I noticed that the topaz was back in her eyes—"because one of them will be dummy, so there'll be three *wise* men. I'll think up something to explain it, of course, or would you let people guess?"

I said that maybe something to explain it would be best.

"Maybe," she said. "And look," she went on, "if you'll give me your home address I'll send you one, because you really gave me the idea."

I said it would be very kind of her.

"No," she said, "I'd like to, because actually I've been thinking and you're absolutely right. Christmas cards ought to be cute and personal, but they ought to be about Christmas too. Traditional. And this one covers everything—only you won't tell it to anyone else, will you, not before next Christmas? Promise? Cross your heart?"

I crossed my heart.

MOMENTUM

*I*t was a lovely day for flying—clear and bright—and for once everything had gone according to schedule. There had been no delay in starting from New York, we had a tail wind, and were flying with incredible smoothness. Los Angeles was only a couple of hours away, and I would have dozed had it not been for a young man across from me who was telling his life story to a stranger held captive in the window seat next to him. He had one of those unaccented voices that carries its monotony far, and by the time he was ready to enter Amherst I had had enough of it, and left my own comfortable seat to escape to the lounge section in the back of the plane, where I hoped his droning would not reach. It was quiet enough there. There was a small man reading a paperback thriller, a larger man, breathing heavily over a map, and a man and a girl sitting silently side by side. The man was heavy with soft fat, and he had the kind of pink skin that sometimes goes with red hair. There was a barbered look about him—a suggestion of friction and hot towels and frequent massage—and, while he was not smoking, he had the look of having just put down a bitten cigar. The girl beside him was very fair, with a bushy fringe held in place by a white veil depending from a tiny flowered hat. Her lips were reddened, and her nose was white with powder, yet there was something about her that was not entirely mature. Her dress gave me no clue—it was the sort of light summer silk that is worn by old and young alike— her slippers were white, the heels neither high nor low, but in her ungloved hands she held a purse that was furry and worn and bore a strong resemblance to Peter Rabbit. It was a child's purse, and I looked again at the man beside her, bulging in ready-made hound's tooth, and an un-accountable resentment of any relationship between them stirred in me. As if he had become aware of it, the man muttered something, hoisted himself from his seat, and went lumbering back to the middle of the plane, leaving the girl alone. She sat quite still, her feet crossed, her hands buried in her rabbity purse. I half smiled at her, but she looked past me, out to where the clouds were beginning to turn pink. I would have returned to my own place, but the insist-ent monologue that had brought me to the lounge still came faintly over the thrum of the plane, and I decided to wait. "I'll give him until he flunks graduation," I told myself. "By then we should be almost in Los Angeles." It wouldn't be too long, I knew, because the stewardess was coming through the body of the plane with a tray of glasses and two cocktail shakers. "Martini or Manhattan," she asked me with that bright smile that never reaches the eyes. I took a Martini, and she addressed the girl with the flowered hat. "Martini or Manhattan," she repeated. The girl looked at the tray. "Could I have some milk?" she asked.

The stewardess held her smile steady. "I'll go see," she said. "We usually carry it for babies." She meant nothing by the remark, but the girl flushed, and I decided to speak to her. "It is a little early for cocktails," I said. She met my eyes for the first time.

"I could have sherry," she said to me when the stewardess had gone, "but my mother says not cocktails until I'm sixteen."

My mind whirled a little, and I had to adjust my impressions.

"Your mother is right, of course," I said. "Is she here on the plane with you?"

"No," she said.

It was a rebuff, but my curiosity rose above it. "Your father, then? Wasn't that your father beside you just now?"

Her eyes traveled over me, not entirely with liking. "The fat man? I don't even know who he is. He was just sitting there," she said.

I felt foolish, but relieved, and thankfully dismissed him from my mind.

"My father is in Hollywood," said the girl. "I'm going out to visit him."

"How nice," I said.

"I'm going to visit my father and my father's wife," she said. "My mother—my real mother—is sending me," and though she still held herself away from me, she volunteered a little more.

"I don't know my father's wife," she said, "but my mother says divorces shouldn't make people uncivilized."

"That's very sensible," I said.

"She has a new baby. I mean my father's wife has," said the child. "He's my half-brother, my mother told me. I have a present for him."

"What fun to have a little brother," I said.

She pushed at her nose veil. "Half-brother," she said. "Of course he's only a baby."

The stewardess came with a glass of milk, and the child, as I now thought of her, took it without looking up; then, as if someone had prodded her, she spoke politely.

"Thank you," she said, and I had a feeling that once she had been taught to curtsy. She drank a little of the milk, and sat holding the glass. "I've never been to Hollywood before," she said, "have you?"

I said, yes, I had been there several times. "It's very interesting, the first time," I said. "And if you're interested in movies, there are tours of the studios that you can take."

"My father can take me," she said. "My father acts in pictures. He's not a star," she said, "but he's very well known."

"How wonderful!" I said.

"I guess so," she said, "but he'd rather direct pictures or write them." She drank from her glass, slowly. "My father's wife writes books, but my mother, my real mother, is an actress." She finished her milk. "Writing isn't like acting, is it?" she asked me then.

I said, no, it wasn't.

"You can look like any old thing and write, but you have to look beautiful to act, don't you?"

I said that it was always a help.

"My mother looks perfectly beautiful even when she isn't acting," the child said, "even when she wakes up in the morning she looks perfectly beautiful, no matter how late she stays up."

Just then, the plane, which had been so steady, lurched and plunged at the same time, taking my stomach with it, and I thought it better to get back to the reassurance of my safety belt.

"I hope you'll have a wonderful visit," I said, as I left. But she was looking out at the clouds again and did not answer.

When we came down at Los Angeles I looked for her, but she lingered in the back of the plane and I did not see her again until I was outside the airport, waiting for a taxi. Then I saw her coming toward me with a slight man in unobtrusive tweeds. He had a lean pleasant face, and he kept his eyes down as people do when they want to pass unnoticed, but from the turned heads and murmurs that followed him it was obvious that he was very well known indeed. At the curb, they were met by a woman who was bareheaded and sunburned, and who had a friendly look. The three of them got into an open sports car, and as they drove away I had a last glimpse of the child sitting stiff and erect between the two adults, her hands clutching her furry purse.

Two weeks later my business in Hollywood was finished and as the quickest way home I had myself booked on an evening plane that would get me to New York early the next morning. I like night flying, anyway. I like the dimness inside and the dark outside and the thought of hours and miles passing unnoticed while I sleep. The plane was full when I boarded it, except for one seat not far from me. The passengers were almost all male, and I studied my seat mate warily, but he seemed as anxious as I was to avoid conversation, so I stowed my bag at my feet, tightened my seat belt, and sought to adjust my chair. I was reaching for my bag again, to get out the slippers that I like to wear on night planes, when there was a stir in the aisle, and I saw a man come in hurriedly, steering a child of fourteen or so. I recognized him at once, but I was not sure of the girl. Then I saw a familiar furry purse, and I realized that this was the child that I had flown with on the way out. Her skin was free of make-up, and was rosy from the sun, but the greatest change was that the bushy fringe was gone. Her hair had been cut in a childish, swirling bob to frame her face endearingly, and it gleamed from brushing, and care.

Her father kissed her once, said a word or two to the hovering stewardess, and was gone. The door closed on him, and almost immediately we started for the runway.

The child had taken the last remaining seat, but once we were airborne the stewardess came to mine. "The young lady's father asked me to look out for her," she said, still glowing from contact with celebrity. "If this gentleman beside you would consent to change, she might be more comfortable with a lady." The gentleman beside me consented with unflattering alacrity, and the change was accomplished. I gave the child the window seat, the stewardess brought her a pillow and blanket, and in a moment she was fast asleep. Even the passing of sandwiches and coffee and fruit did not waken her, and from time to time during the night I opened my eyes to see her still sleeping, her lashes like gold shadows on her cheeks.

Morning came, and with it the stir of breakfast trays and people moving stiffly to the washrooms. The sky was still gray outside, as though the day were only an uncertain promise. The child beside me turned restlessly, yawned, and was awake.

"Good morning," I said.

She looked at me without enthusiasm. "You don't remember me," I said, "but we flew out together."

"Did we?" she said, and looked out of the window where as yet there was nothing to see.

I left her, and went to make what I could of myself after the cramped night, with cold water and powder and lipstick. When I came back she turned to me from the window. "I don't see how you knew me," she said. "I look all different now."

"I knew you," I said.

"My hair's been cut," she said.

"I noticed it," I said. "It's very pretty. Don't you like it?"

"I did out there," she said, and frowned. "My father had it done. And my father's wife got me new clothes. Shorts and things."

"You liked *those*, didn't you?" I asked her.

"I did out there," she said again, and turned back to the window.

The stewardess came by with breakfast trays which we both refused.

"I want to have my breakfast with my mother," the child said.

I said that I wanted to have mine at home, too, and she nodded curtly. I felt that I should have let her alone, but some need to reach her impelled me to go on. I asked her if she had had a nice visit.

"I guess so," she said.

"And what about your new little brother?" I asked.

"My half-brother," she corrected me. "I didn't see much

of him. He has regular hours for everything. It was all very regular. My father's wife has everything that way."

"Didn't you like that?"

"I did out there," she said with no expression, "but my mother, my real mother, says it's silly to be tied to time. She just has things when we feel like it."

"Well," I said, "with a new baby in the house there has to be a schedule, and I expect your father's work has to be considered."

"He wasn't working while I was there," she said. "He had two weeks between pictures, that's why he could have me."

"Did you like Hollywood?" I asked her.

"It's very easy out there," she said. "Everybody's always working."

"Oh?" I said.

"I mean, everyone you *meet* is working. But my mother's going to work soon. She's going into a new play."

"How wonderful," I said.

"It isn't really," she answered, as if she were being patient with my ignorance. "It isn't a very good play, but my mother is doing it because we have to make money. It's just a plain play, and my mother would rather be in one where she could sing or dance. But we have to make money." She looked at me, as if wondering if I would understand. "Of course, my father sends us money, too, but my mother says it goes so fast."

I said yes, indeed it did. "And maybe the play will be fun after all," I added.

"It's because we have to make money," she said, and turned to the window again, dismissing me.

I said no more until she spoke again, of her own accord. "My father gave me tennis lessons," she said, as if to no one.

"You know," I said, "I think you really must have had a lovely time out there."

She twisted in her seat. "They were always talking about schools," she said. "As if my mother couldn't teach me everything."

I didn't answer that.

"And they gave me a lot of books," she told me. "My father is very edurite. Very well read," she explained. "My father's wife is, too, and they want me to be."

She was half resentful, half wistful.

"They sound very nice," I said, trying to help her. "Giving you books, and teaching you tennis; I'm sure you must have liked it a lot."

"I liked it when I was there," she said, still without emphasis. She took a small mirror from her rabbit purse and examined herself in the increasing light. "Do you think my *mother* will like my hair?" she asked, and now there was a hint of anxiety in her voice.

"I'm sure she will," I said.

She put the mirror back and reached into a carryall that was at her feet and brought out a book. I recognized it as being high on the best-seller list, its dust jacket torridly proclaiming its pseudo-historical content.

"Do you have a pen," she asked me, "or a pencil?"

I had a pen, and I gave it to her. "Thank you," she said, with the same oddly prompted politeness with which she had thanked the stewardess for the milk, and opened the book at its flyleaf. She considered it for a while, and then began to write slowly and with great care, her head bent, her hair shining in the sun that had risen to flood the plane. When she had done, she touched my arm, and gave me back my pen. She waited and then spoke, and for the first time she spoke to me as a child to an adult.

"I'm bringing this to my mother," she said. She handed me the book. "Would you look at what I have written and tell me if it's all right?"

I read the inscription in its sturdy unformed writing.

"To my mother this book from her loving daughter. As a momentum of a happy homecoming."

"Is it all right?" she asked again. "If you were my mother, would you like it?"

I had to wait a moment before I could reply. "If I were your mother, I would love it," I said.

She took the book from me and put it in her bag. "My

father said perfume, but I got a book," she said, "because my mother is edurite, too."

The "No Smoking" sign went on, and we fastened our seat belts. The plane circled and lost altitude, we banked over the airport, our ears filled, and we were down.

Once more I lost sight of the child as we left the plane, but as I reached the gate I turned and saw her coming. I had half expected that she would be running, but she was walking slowly, her carryall slung from one shoulder. As she came nearer I saw that she had pulled her hair over her forehead in some semblance of its former look, and she was holding her rabbit purse tight with both hands.

Date Due